I0733919

Antifa Lit Journal
Volume 2
Hungry Work

Published in the United States by
Not a Pipe Publishing Ink-Corporated, LLC
Independence, Oregon.
www.NotAPipePublishing.com

Paperback Edition

ISBN-13: 978-1-956892-81-9

Cover by Benjamin Gorman

Contents

Introduction

by Benjamin Gorman

I recently received a thoughtful letter from an author who was concerned about working with Not a Pipe Publishing because we published (and will continue to publish) the *Antifa Lit Journal*. Donald Trump's executive order to declare Antifa a terrorist organization had made the author rightly nervous. It is scary.

The individuals who publish, write, and support the journal do identify as Antifa. But Antifa is an ideological principle, not an organization. It's an abbreviation for anti-fascist. Thus, Antifa is not a singular organization but a descriptor. When placed before a noun, it functions as an adjective. Consequently, an organization can be anti-fascist, but anti-fascism cannot be an organization, just as an organization can be large or small, but we can't say "small" is an organization. That wouldn't make any sense. In fact, the journal's title has two adjectives, both of which are abbreviations. Both "Antifa" and "Lit" modify "Journal." Can we even imagine how absurd it would sound if the President declared "Lit" to be a terrorist organization, counting on his base to fail to know (and expecting collaborating journalists to fail to clarify) that "Lit" stands for "Literary"?

Unfortunately, that doesn't seem as impossible as it once did.

The absurdity of calling something which isn't an organization a "terrorist organization" is not without consequence. This gives huge latitude to the Executive to attack individuals who it disagrees with. We've seen this same danger with the term "terrorist." What is a terrorist? A person who causes terror, right? We all envision people who cause horrific acts of violence. But we have also seen that once a government has the power to label anyone it wants a "terrorist" (or, even more broadly, a "terrorist sympathizer"), this can extend to just about anyone the government doesn't like.

I want to be very clear about this: Not a Pipe Publishing has never advocated for violence or illegality of any kind. Opposing fascism takes many forms. The soldiers who stormed the beaches of Normandy were all opposing fascism, so obviously anti-fascism can become violent, but Not a Pipe has never called for violence, nor does it promote it. In my own writing, I have called for acts of civil disobedience, like wildcat strikes and blocking traffic. Some people will feel that goes too far, and they'll draw the line at anything which breaks any law. I disagree. But being anti-fascist is not advocacy for violence or terrorism. It's a call to end state-sponsored mass violence and stochastic terrorism inspired by a fascist movement.

So now we have a term, "Antifa" (which many people don't know merely means anti-fascist), labeled erroneously as an organization. And it's been joined to a term associating it with people who blow up buildings. Again, it should be laughably absurd, but the consequences are very real.

Organizations and individuals associated with terrorism can have their assets frozen.

They can be charged in criminal cases (though the government has historically tried to avoid real trials because actual discussions of evidence don't tend to be flattering to the government).

They can be imprisoned without trial.

And, because our government declared war on "terrorism," those slapped with the label can even be targets of the most powerful military on Earth. In fact, even those who have nothing to do with the individual can be blown up for standing too close to someone labeled a terrorist, and those victims are considered "collateral damage," not human beings murdered by a government at war with an imprecise word.

So yes, we share the author's concern. It should scare all of us when a President can unilaterally decide to threaten enemies and has the power to cause so much harm.

This concern should be even greater when the supposed enemy is the ideological principle of anti-fascism. And that's because, when it comes to fascism, there is a true binary. One either supports or opposes fascism. There is no in between. So when the President says Antifa is the enemy, this is as close as I expect we will ever get to an open declaration of fascist rule, and it makes everyone who opposes him a potential target.

This specifically endangers Not a Pipe Publishing Ink-Corporated LLC, a legal entity headquartered in the United States. And it increases the danger for all the authors, poets, and artists who choose to work with us.

I could choose to try and change our values to appear more subservient to the regime, but the Internet is eternal, and, frankly, I couldn't live with myself if I compromised my values in that way. I do understand others have to make their own calculations based on their own unique situations and their values. I chose to move to a different country, in large part so I could publish a journal that is explicitly anti-fascist and publish books by authors who want to continue to speak out. It was not an easy decision, and it was a more difficult sacrifice than most people recognize. Some people seem to think we are rich and privileged. They do not understand that we made a calculation that it's better to be broke than to be dead.

Not a Pipe is committed to being an activist press. As long as I own it, the company will do its best to promote marginalized voices, to be antiracist and feminist, and yes, to be anti-fascist. Just as I made a calculation that I'd prefer to be broke and physically safe rather than living amongst people who wanted to kill me, I've made an ethical calculation that I would prefer to have my American company fail if the United States becomes a place where people cannot safely disagree with their government rather than have an American company succeed by catering to a fascist regime.

Thank you, Dear Reader, for supporting the amazing artists who are included in this collection, and for supporting our commitment to anti-fascism with your resources, time, and energy. The danger of the rise of fascism around the world is underestimated by too many. I'm honestly not sure if enough people will take the threat seriously to prevent greater horrors. But you give me hope.

-Benjamin Gorman
Publisher, Not a Pipe Publishing Ink-Corporated LLC
Co-Editor, the *Antifa Lit Journal*

certainly

by Maia Justine Storm

certainly we have no stuffed cattle cars
no gas chambers at track's end
no crematoria
certainly we can make no comparisons.
but still.
there is a whiff, no?
a slight resonance in the back of one's heart

masked men grabbing people off the
street, out of the courthouse,
even out of the bloody abattoir

last week Chaofeng Ge
32 years old, Chinese, hung himself
in a Pennsylvania jail.

shall we remember his name

The First Christian Republic of America

by Carrie Schweiger

Justice Mather tugged the black cap over the Puritan wig the republic required all judges to wear. A decade had passed since the big change, and he still didn't like the silly-looking wigs. He missed making judgments with an unadorned head. His scalp sweated and itched under the thing, muddling his thoughts. Such a small price, the discomfort. One he'd pay a million times to have the world they had now. A government devoted to Christ.

He adjusted his robe and picked up the tablet loaded with all the accusations and evidence he needed to rule the day's cases.

"You stand accused of neglecting your ovulating-congenial duties," he said to Defendant 1515, "failing to have dinner prepared by the time your husband returns from work, and ignoring your household cleaning duties. How do you plead?"

"Not guilty."

"You'll address me as your honor." *The insolence.* "I'm obligated to remind you that evidence of your crimes was collected from your phone, smart appliances, and computer. You still wish to enter a not-guilty plea?"

"I do. Your Honor."

The defendant's tone was anything but respectful. Justice Mather would not let a woman get the best of him, especially not a reformed one. "Why attempt a not-guilty plea if the evidence is against you?"

"May I speak, Your Honor?"

Much better. "You may."

"When I was assigned a spouse, the state promised the hormone treatments would cure my husband and I of our," she cleared her throat—the reformed ones always did at this point, "unnatural tendencies."

"It's a scientifically proven fact."

"In our case, it has left us with no desire for each other. Anyone, for that matter. We live as brother and sister. As such, I have no responsibilities to him."

"According to the law, you are his wife and caretaker."

"Even after the law forced us to marry on the threat of torture and death…"

Judge Mather scrambled to press the button, interrupting the live feed. No need to give the viewership ideas; didn't want the public thinking they could reject the new ways.

Defendant 1515 was still speaking. "I do not believe the scripture would sanctify such a marriage."

Judge Mather depressed the button. "Gracefully, God doesn't ask your opinion. And the law does not care nor need it either." He pounded the gavel. "The court finds you guilty, and charges you to--"

"Your Honor, my husband and I wish to take service."

Judge Mather jammed the button again. Hopefully, he'd gotten it before she claimed service. The elders hated when defendants pleaded for service. They needed more babies to replace the dwindling population, not more nuns and monks.

"Your husband is here?" Judge Mather didn't dare lift his finger from the button.

"Obviously. Your Honor. He's the only one allowed in the courtroom with me."

So disrespectful. Had she not claimed service, he would have sentenced her to at least ten years' solemn labor, followed by a lifetime of sincere devotion.

The husband was all arms and legs. "Please stand." Judge Mather's finger ached from holding the button down. "You wish to enter service?"

"I do."

"Both of you understand, you will relinquish the freedoms of this world and will live in complete service to the Lord."

"We do."

Why did they always sound so eager? All they did was tend gardens, study the holy word, eat bland food, and pray? It sounded dreadful. "From this day until the Lord calls you home, you will be pledged to the convent or monastery of your choosing."

"I pledge to St. Cuthbert's," the husband said.

"I pledge to the Holy Heart." Defendant 1515 smirked. The reformed ones always did that too when they pledged to Holy Heart. Perhaps the elders should pay them a visit. He made a mental note to bring it up at the next council meeting. If they found something, it would raise him in their graces, and Judge Wyatt would no longer be a threat.

"Once you leave this room, a guard will escort you to your new homes." Judge Mather released the button and pounded his gavel. "The law is the law, and the law is divine. Dismissed."

The doors to the courtroom opened. Six guards carrying assault rifles escorted Defendant 1515 and her husband out of the room, leaving Judge Mather, the Bailiff, and the court stenographer alone in the room. *Good riddance.*

Why the elders ever allowed service was beyond him. It was too medieval for his taste. But what did he know? He was a mere enforcer of the law God handed to the holy leaders. Judge Mather scrolled to the next case and began reviewing the evidence.

Bailiff Hawkins cleared his throat. "Your Honor."

"Yes?" Judge Mather said without looking up from the screen.

"There was a problem with the live feed."

"What do you mean, problem?"

"The feed aired even after you pressed the button."

"What?" His chest tightened, sending tension down his arms.

"I assured the elders you pressed the button. And it wasn't your fault. That the buttons malfunction from time to time."

"Of course, it wasn't my fault." The elders had to believe he had performed his duty. To think what they'd do if they didn't. He shuddered. How Judge Wyatt would just love to take this seat. "Why didn't you stop me?"

"We're not supposed to interrupt a ruling, except in an emergency."

"This was an emergency."

"The elders didn't think so. I'm to replace the button."

The elders *didn't* think so. Judge Mather rolled his chair away from the bench, taking the tablet with him. Their ways rarely made sense, but he knew better than to voice his thoughts.

Bailiff Hawkins quickly replaced the button and called in the next defendant.

The man who entered was short and built like a bulldog. Around his neck were the scars of tattoo removal. The telltale sign of a reluctant convert. Given his offense, it would seem, he remained reluctant.

The door slammed shut. Bailiff Hawkins started the proceeding with a prayer and approached Defendant 1516 with a Bible. The man gave his oath. "I swear to tell the whole truth, so help me God. The law is the law, and the law is divine."

Once the ceremony concluded, Judge Mather began, "You've been accused of neglecting to thank the Lord for his generosity before each meal; thus, leaving your family open to attacks from Satan. How do you plea?"

"Not guilty, Your Honor."

"You're aware these accusations came to the court from video evidence?"

"There must be some mistake, Your Honor. I always lead my family in prayer."

Judge Mather cued the evidence. "This is you, correct?"

The video showed the family grabbing food and dispersing to separate rooms in the house without a single prayer uttered.

"It looks like me. But it's not. Someone must have tampered with the devices in my house. AI malfunction, perhaps."

Malfunction, indeed. The video feeds ran through the best anti-AI filters. It wouldn't do to have some computer wiz fake their religious duties. "That is impossible, sir."

"Then the devices malfunctioned. They've been known to do so from time to time."

Something he knew all too well. But that wasn't the case here. Judge Mather leaned forward. "You are lying to the court. And doing a poor job at it. Now the court has the authority to grant leniency against such offenses if you confess your sins and beg our Lord's forgiveness."

Defendant 1516 hung his head and fidgeted with his thumbs.

"If you refuse to confess, the court is inclined to give you 36 months of solemn labor, followed by 48 months of divine devotion."

"It is me," Defendant 1516 said, his shoulder sagging. "Please forgive me, Your Honor. I didn't mean to lie or neglect my duties. Work has been stressful."

"That does not give you the right to forget your prayers. As the spiritual leader of the household, you are responsible for your family. Failing to properly shepherd your children will leave them vulnerable to the devil's temptation. You do not want them to end up before me one day or burn in the fires of hell because of your neglect. Now do you?"

"No, Your Honor."

"From the video evidence, I declare you guilty. I sentence you to 120 days of sincere devotion."

"But, Your Honor, my work. I'm already so far behind."

"You should have thought of that before you broke the law. The law is the law, and the law is divine. Dismissed. Next."

Defendant 1516 was escorted from the room. Defendant 1517 was brought in. She was tall with a trim athletic body. No sign of the bookworm her case suggested she was. One never could tell, though.

Bailiff Hawkins swore her in.

"You stand accused of reading illegal material and watching forbidden movies. How do you plea?"

"Hearsay, Your Honor."

Judge Mather rubbed his temple. "I don't think you understand how this works.

I read the charge. You say 'guilty' or 'not guilty'."

"But it is hearsay, Your Honor."

"The video evidence begs to differ..." Judge Mather searched for the link to the evidence but found none. "Bailiff Hawkins, it appears the link to the evidence is broken. Would you kindly fix it?"

Bailiff Hawkins touched the screen. "There is no video evidence, Your Honor."

"How unusual." Judge Mather tapped his finger against the tablet. What was the defendant supposedly reading? *The Great Gatsby. 1984. The Lord of the Rings. A Wizard of Earthsea. Beloved. Parable of the Sower.* In the world before, he had enjoyed them all. Occasionally, he longed for the old movies and books. Not the vulgar ones, of course. But the ones with real grit. Much better than the wholesome Pollyanna entertainment they were allowed now. Oh well, the law is the law, and the law is divine. "As your case is a matter of hearsay, you are entitled to a trial by a jury of your peers. You will wait at the Sisters of the Holy Cross Covent until your appointed day. Do you have any questions?"

"How long must I wait at the Holy Cross?"

Judge Mather tapped the tablet screen. "Trials are about three years out. Any other questions?"

"Will the jury include women?"

"Don't be glib, Defendant 1517. I have the authority to rule in your case. Save you all that waiting."

"Sorry, Your Honor."

"The Lord will forgive you. The law is the law, and the law is divine. Dismissed. Next."

This one looked every bit the troublemaker her record made her out to be. Her hair was tangled and uneven. Not in the tidy bun respectable women wear. Her face looked like it hadn't been washed in days. It was covered in both dirt and grime. Her unwashed state was from living on the run, if the scent rolling off of her was any indication. This was perhaps the first time he'd ever smelled a defendant from where they stood. Even her prison uniform was wrinkled and dirty. When Judge Mather squinted, he detected dirt under her fingernails.

Bailiff Hawkins prayed, held out the Bible, and asked her to place her hand on it to swear in.

She kept her hands at her side and stared forward; her eyes focused on a spot below the high seat.

"Defendant 1518, you are to swear on the Bible before we begin," Judge Mather warned.

The girl kept her gaze fixed.

"The court will have to hold you in contempt if you refuse." He huffed. "You might as well do as you're expected. Or we will compel you to swear in."

"I refuse to acknowledge a book of fables." The corner of the girl's lip turned up as she finished. So, she was one of *those*.

He raised an eyebrow and nodded to Bailiff Hawkins who motioned for another court guard to assist him. He prodded the girl with his electric rod. She grimaced but didn't cry out, didn't move her gaze. Hawkins forced her hand on the Bible as the guard moved the girl's jaw to mimic the words of the oath.

Judge Mather scrolled through her record. "It says your first sentence came a month after the republic was formed. For..." he adjusted his glasses, "cursing the Lord and his appointed emissaries. You were given 100 days of solemn labor and 200 days of sincere devotion. During sincere devotion, you attacked one of the prayer leaders." He tsked. "Given 500 days of solemn labor and 700 days of sincere devotion. My, my."

He continued to list her transgressions against the Lord's State—for they were now one and the same. She'd spent most of her life since the establishment of Christ's republic in one form of penitence or another. It took some people so long to see the light.

"You're here because you ran from your solemn labor. Where were you running to, my child?"

Her gaze flicked to his face. It was the first time she looked away from the spot on the bench. The burning hatred in her eyes sent him back in his high seat. "Well, child." He had to speak to keep her from thinking she'd unnerved him. "Where were you going?"

"Anywhere that wasn't fucking here."

Damn. He hadn't gotten to the button in time. The elders would dock him for letting that word slip to the viewership. "And how do you plea?"

"That I belong in the world before." In one swift motion, Defendant 1518 slipped a match from her robe, struck it against the bench, and set herself aflame. "God Bless the U.S.A."

Judge Mather froze in his chair, horrified. She stared at him, defiance strong in her gaze. Then the screaming, smell of burned flesh and hair followed.

"Sir. Your Honor." Hawkins ran toward the girl who'd fallen to the floor. "The button."

"Oh, dear. Recess." Judge Mather scrambled to hit the button. A great roaring sounded in his ears and his head.

The sprinklers went off, drenching everything. Too late to save the burned girl. Her eyes starred, unseeing, out of her blackened flesh.

Hawkins and the other guards ushered him out of the courtroom. Outside they took out handcuffs. "Let me see your wrists, sir."

"What?" Judge Mather was still shaken by what had he'd just seen. Why would Hawkins want to look at his wrists? Had the fire singed them? Is that why there was the great roaring in his head?

"Hold out your wrists," Bailiff Hawkins said, unlocking the handcuffs.

"But? No." Understanding finally quieted the great roaring. "I've been a loyal, faithful servant to the Lord these many years."

"I'm sorry, sir. I only follow orders. Orders are law, and the law is divine. And all that."

Mather held out his arms. He would show the elders his faithfulness. They'd see it and remember his years of service. He might receive a few days of sincere devotion. Only fitting for failing to protect the viewership from the horrors he'd just witnessed.

His damp robes weighed on him as they waited for the robots to clean and clear the room. The scent of smoke hung heavy on his shoulders and stung his nose hairs. Would he ever be rid of it?

The doors to the court opened, and Bailiff Hawkins led him inside. This time to the defendant's docket. It was a view he never expected to see.

The floor showed no sign of the violence that had happened earlier. If only his mind could be so easily wiped clean.

Judge Wyatt sat in the high chair vacated by Mather. The judge refused to meet Mather's eyes. This was not a good turn of events. In the world before, Mather often excelled where Wyatt failed. The man had sworn he held no grudge. That it was before the Lord had redeemed the country. But Mather always sensed Wyatt was waiting to strike.

Bailiff Hawkins held out the Bible and asked Mather to swear upon. "I swear to tell the whole truth, nothing but the truth. So help me God." *Please God.* "The law is the law, and the law is divine." For some reason the words seemed to burn as he spoke them.

Judge Wyatt cleared his throat. "Defendant 1519, you're accused of a very serious crime. One of the most serious I've heard before."

Mather laughed. He couldn't help.

"You think it's funny," Judge Wyatt said.

"Your Honor. I understand I was slow to end the transmission and allowed the viewership to see something no one should see. But that's hardly a serious offense."

"Your crime is conspiring with the forces of evil to harm the Lord's republic."

"I would never." A gavel hammered against Mather' chest. This had to be a mistake. The elders knew his devotion.

"Only speak when asked a direct question."

"But I'm innocent. The record shows that I love Christ as much as any man and have done nothing against his republic. The law is the law, and the law is divine."

Judge Wyatt leaned forward. "You expect this court to believe you hold the law divine, and yet you permitted the flock to watch a deranged criminal defile the Lord's holy chamber."

"It was a mistake. It happened so suddenly." Judge Mather clasped his hands together. "Please, Your Honor. Show mercy on the Lord's faithful servant."

"Mercy?" Judge Wyatt's lips twitched, causing a shudder to run through Mather. "This court finds you guilty. I sentence you to 5,000 days of solemn labor followed by 10,000 days sincere devotion. The law is the law, and the law is divine."

"That's harsher than any ruling in this court before." The words were out before Mather could stop them. The ruling amounted to a death sentence. He didn't deserve such cruel treatment, especially when he'd given so much for Christ and the republic.

"Which is why the Lord saw to make me this court's judge."

"But, please. I—"

"Defendant 1519, you are dismissed." Judge Wyatt turned his attention to the tablet. "Next."

Meteoright

by Allan Lake

I've been Unfriended
by an old acquaintance
in his moment of righteous
decisiveness or something.
Said he had noticed hints
of what's Left (as he awaits
the end of the world) and
called me a woke 'Globalist'.
Despite being from the flat
prairie, like my ex-friend,
it's true that I believe
the world is round.
I stand exposed.

Just Desserts

by Flavian Mark Lupinetti

My brother Franco points out the parallels.
All three of us:
    Italian kids,
      high school wrestlers and valedictorians,
      documented beefs with insurance companies.
Fitting the profile so well,
shouldn't you and I take offense
nobody considered us suspects?

Franco ticks another box.
The Baltimore connection.
Luigi was a native,
but we went to school there.
I wonder if he's an Orioles fan like us.
If he beats the rap, shouldn't the O's
let him throw out the first pitch next season?

Yet as an assistant DA, Franco has empathy for the prosecutors.
How will they ever pick a jury?
'Do you have health insurance? You can't be impartial.'
'Can you not afford health insurance? Get outta here.'
'Are you a doctor, a nurse, a physician assistant? Beat it.'
They might not be able to find twelve people
in a town the size of New York who would vote to convict.

Franco has given this a lot of thought.

Don't tell me this didn't change anything.
The companies' web sites used to flaunt photos
of their executives--soft focus, opulent settings--
like those portraits of J.P. Morgan, Jay Gould, John D. Rockefeller.
Now, even the names on the web sites have disappeared.

I try convincing Franco it was wrong to kill the guy like that,
even if the dude's body count surpassed that of Netanyahu.
Shooting motherfuckers the way Luigi did--
one at a time--
is so darn inefficient.

Dressed for the Occasion

by Amanda Cherry

The fabric isn't as nice as it looked on the website. That's the risk you take when shopping online, I guess.

The box is nice. A Black-on-Black logo on heavy pasteboard—a tight-fitting lid, a custom foil sticker. All the trappings of getting what I paid for, at least.

But the fabric.... It doesn't look high-end. I was hoping for a more refined appearance. The material has a sheen to it—it reminds me of cheap polyester that's been pressed with a too-hot iron. I do suppose that could be a feature; a peon in a cheap suit can fly under most people's radar. An obviously expensive suit could draw attention. I didn't buy this suit for looks, anyway.

The sleeves are loose, the shoulders extra wide, but not enough to constitute an ill fit. I can move in this suit. I can hurl a brick or throw a punch. I can reach above me to pull down a banner touting hate. I can paint over a malicious slogan even when it's over my head. I can take the hood off a Klansman if he dares to get that close.

The trousers are strange- nipped in at the waist with room in the seat. The knees are reinforced; I can feel that from the inside, but there's no outward indication. If pushed to the ground, my trousers won't tear. They're loose enough to run in and the length is just as I ordered.

Even in the midst of a fracas, I could move in and out of a crowd and look like nothing more than a bystander. It could be an ordinary suit.

It could be.

The pockets zip shut, and they lock, should anyone wish to search them, they will be in for a fight. Hidden tabs in the cuffs at both my wrists and ankles seal the lining to my skin—an extra precaution should that become necessary. It's all the protection one might want from acid, or gas, or anything meant to scald.

That's the sheen.

This suit, this cheap-looking custom masterpiece, is riot-proof.

The hidden headpiece is the finishing touch. With Velcro closures, it dons quickly, making my ears, chin, nose, and forehead equally steeled against whatever may come. The facemask filters particles. When this final piece is deployed, my only exposed skin will be my eyes and hands—a situation easily remedied by carrying gloves and goggles.

Gloves are easy; they're ordinary and mundane. Anyone might be carrying gloves. Goggles are harder—conspicuous. I will wear my glasses, then. Keep goggles in a briefcase. There's a chance I could be caught without them, a condition I will likely regret with some intensity should I encounter a true need for eye protection.

But it's a risk I'm willing to take.

Any visible lump could betray me as someone who doesn't belong.

And I can't have that.

I won't run that risk.

The point of the suit is to be inconspicuous—to walk among them. Because these men wear suits. These men with their cries of supremacy and destabilization: they wear suits made of wool and gabardine, of silk and cashmere. Suits that contain their hate, their lies, and their machinations.

Most of us—we don't wear suits. We wear cargo pants, bandanas and worn-out shoes. We wear calluses on our hands and sweat on our brows. We wear scowls and ball caps and aprons and smocks. We wear tattoos of the names of those we love who the policies concocted by the men in suits have taken from us. And we wear our anger—and our outrage—with pride.

But they wear suits. And so now, so will I.

I will wear my suit and I will haunt their halls. I will listen to their speeches and I will abide their vitriolic repartee. I will bide my time and I will learn their ways.

I will keep my enemies close.

Because when we rise up—and we will rise up—I will draw first blood. Their reckoning is coming, and when it does I will be in their midst. I will wind up my fist and I will fight, not on the side of the men in suits, but on the side of justice and of right.

The Resistance is coming, and the regime will fall. The oligarchs will have no quarter. Their tears will flood the streets through which our peaceful marches were once rebuked by violence.

We will give back to them the pain they have so freely visited upon us.

And there I'll be on the front line, standing proudly, perfectly dressed for the occasion.

Suprem(acist) Court
by Beulah Vega

The anti-anxiety meds are barely holding
off panic as each new (single judge-authored)
writ arrives

Days turn to night to a weird liminal time
where emergency sessions create shadows
moving liberty backwards and driving authoritarianism
forward at the speed of a bullet train, screaming

along the legacy lines of long-dead
robber barons, carpet baggers, and slave holders.

What dies when only death can free
my country from a 6-3 dissent?
-*Habeas Corpus* is looking pale and weak.

Our souls are being auctioned
with 'fast hammer' gavel strikes
ensuring winning bids before we
(the people) knew that bidding had begun.

Every night now, toothless men in black gowns
slip into the stalls of power - groom
the constitution into an obedient

broken horse. They bleed
its marrow into glue that sticks
the tyrant on his gaudy gilded seat.

In a once rose-scented lawn, life (liberty) has
decayed into the marble and granite sepulcher
of democratic ideals

Sepulcher not tomb
-*Nulla Corpora*- (our bodies are not there)
only our freedoms.

Mr. President, Forget Killing Antifa

by Andres Castro

Choke
metal-jacketed hollow points!

On U.S.

This is no apocalyptic sci-fi movie.
The young know you can't kill

The future is here.
Antifa...

transcendent idea
in Italy's Arditi del Popolo's
against Mussolini's Blackshirts...

Embodied
Resistance

in Germany's Antifaschistische Aktion's
against Hitler's Nazis...

Resistance

in the international brigade's
against Franco in Spain's civil war.

Resistance

Resistance

Leaping

through time...

Space...

to grow here

Now!

Mr. P, forget killing

Antifa...

angry? If this poem   Appears

in an activist project   Will

I become a target
for a lost soul
burning crosses in mind?

                                                       Me?

                                                       Little Gadfly

aiming these bullet points
at your fascist face.

1. Revived Authoritarianism
2. Defended Propaganda
3. Declared Nationalism
4. Unleashed Sexism
5. Erased Human Rights
6. Attacked Scapegoats
7. Suppressed Dissent
8. Enshrined Militarism
9. Unbounded Oligarchy
10. Embraced White Supremacy

How   many   holes   in   you   and   your   legacy
will   history   record?

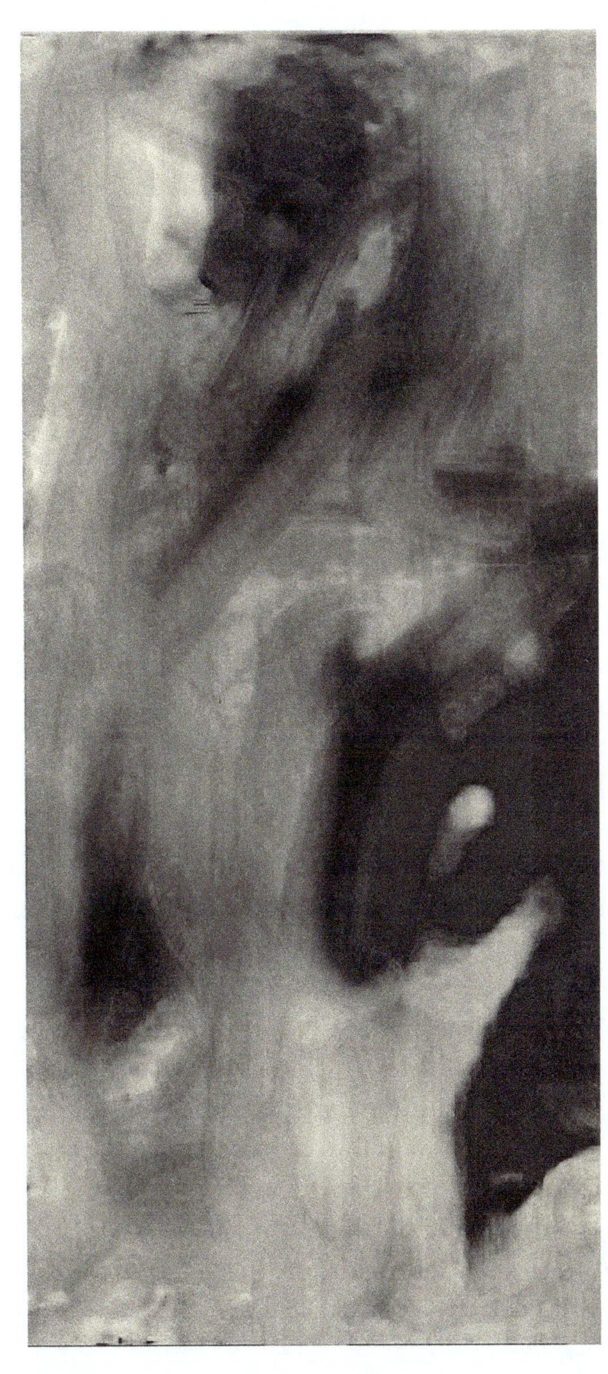

from the series Icons of War

by Tony Brinkley

Papers Please, America's Reflection
"America Tips into Fascism"

by Valdez Hill

The air turns cold
A chill not of winter, but of a coming change
A new kind of dawn
Breaks over our land
Darker than we remember.

The cities once bright
Now shadowed by marching boots
Not our boots, not our town's own guard
But soldiers from afar
Sent by a single will that calls itself a king
Governors, loyal to one man
Send him their armed men
Ready to walk into places
Where other ideas grow
To take them over
To silence the talk and seize the squares
Where free voices once rang.

Federal eyes, sharp and cold
Watch from the shadows
They find the names of those who speak out
Who stand against the rising tide
A knock at the door, not a friend
But a uniform, a badge of the state
Coming for thinkers, for speakers

For anyone who dares to question the king.

Our capital, a place of open doors
Now locked down, a fortress under watch
No one asked for this
No riot, no threat
Just a strange parade of steel and silent might
Green machines, made for war, roll down avenues
Where children once played
Soldiers, rifles held tight
Patrol where tourists once walked
The low roar of engines. the crunch of metal
As these war wagons, big and unyielding
Clash with quiet cars, a sound not of peace
But of occupation, a chilling warning
In the very heart of our home.

Then the street itself changes, a sudden stop
A hard voice, sharp and cold
"Papers please!"
The words hang heavy, a ghost from old stories
From far-off lands
We swore we'd never be
Uniformed men, dark and severe
Blocking your path home, demanding your proof
Your right to just be
A shiver runs down the spine
A memory of fear from history books
Now real, now here in our streets.

And worse, the vans, dark and unmarked
Slide through the night
Masked men appear, like shadows made real
They grab a person, no reason given
No word spoken
Raw force wrestles them down
Into the dark van and it speeds away
No trace, no answer
Families search
Beg for a name

For a place for a sign of life
But find only silence, a black hole
Where a loved one used to be.

The man who once preached
Of small government
Of freedom for business
Now holds it by the throat
His hand outstretched
Not to help, but to take
Companies, big and old, feel his heavy gaze
To earn his smile, to keep their doors open
They must give him a piece
Parts of their work
Portions of their profit
Or face strange new taxes
Made up on the spot
A price for his personal favor
A king's demand
For the right to simply exist, to do honest work
In a land that once called itself free.

This is the face, unveiled and stark
This is the new shape of old nightmares
A crown not worn on the head
But felt in the fear, in the silent streets
In the stolen voices, in the shadow of steel
America, looking back at us, changed
A mirror showing, what we swore
We would never become.

Saying Goodbye

by George Crossman

Rob,

Maybe we should say goodbye in person. This is our chance.

The Maxinkuckee Lake house just sold. New owners already have the keys, but we can always book rooms at Bentley's B & B. There's still time for you and I to have one last sail. Fall colours will be magnificent.

Then my keepsakes and I are leaving for Nijmegen.

Dearest Eileen, please understand.

What's happening is intolerable.

Bless you both and all the best.

-Marilyn

Rob unplugged his laptop then carried it next door to his wife's office. Eileen sat at her desk entering queries and suggestions into the first draft of an economics textbook.

"There's an email from Marilyn. She says she's leaving – for good, I suspect."

Eileen saved her comments into the chapter she'd been editing, then turned as Rob knelt at her feet. "Can I see?" He positioned the screen on her knees.

"Nijmegen's in Holland, isn't it?"

Rob's joints cracked as he leaned backwards onto the carpet. "About an hour southeast from Amsterdam. Marilyn has cousins there."

"No closer family – aunts, uncles, brothers or sisters?"

He shook his head. "Remember, she's an only child? Her parents came to America when she was three. They're long gone, and except for a few visits back home, she's always lived in the U.S."

"Will she apply to be a permanent resident in Holland?"

Rob shrugged. "Probably, if all her paperwork's ready. She renewed her Dutch citizenship last winter."

Eileen shifted the laptop aside and reached out to bring Rob into her arms. "You two have been best friends forever. I understand."

"I need to see her one last time."

"Well, don't bring back that virus. It's still kicking around down there."

From Sarnia, Rob drove west into Michigan, crossing over the Blue Water Bridge. Beside him, east bound traffic re-entering Canada packed the span from shore to shore. At noon, on the American side, he had his pick of empty U.S. custom booths. Choosing a lane at random, he opened his passport and rolled down the window.

"Citizenship?"

"Canadian."

"Really!" The officer bent lower to look into Rob's car, "Your ID says you were born in Pokagon County, Indiana."

"Sir, that was seventy-seven years ago. I've lived in Toronto since 1970."

"Reason for your visit?"

"I'm meeting an old friend."

"Hmmm." The officer drummed the passport with his fingertips. "Did you vote?"

"I'm Canadian, Sir. I'm not eligible to vote in American elections."

"Now, that's not quite what I asked. Is it, Mr. Crossman? Try again. Did you vote?"

"No, Sir. I don't vote in your elections."

"And if I scan the electoral records for Pokagon County, what will I find?"

"Nothing. Nothing at all. I didn't vote."

"As you can see, Mr. Crossman, it's a slow day. Let's take a couple minutes." The guard turned back to his workstation and typed in Crossman's name.

Rob's heart beat in his throat until the officer again looked down into the car. "Well, well. Seems you're telling the truth."

"Yes, of course."

The guard smiled and returned his passport. "You may proceed. But watch when you reach the Indiana border. They'll likely have more questions. Have a good day, Mr. Crossman."

"Are you armed?"

"No, Sir. Certainly not."

Six soldiers in the uniform of the Constitutional Guard blocked the highway at Niles, just before the 'Welcome to Indiana' billboard. His car was the only one waiting to navigate the chicane of chest-high, concrete barriers.

"Step out. Slowly please, Mr. Crossman. Keep your hands up and stand over there. We have to inspect what you're bringing in. Scan him, Larry."

"Take off your belt and shoes," Rob was told, then a metal-detecting wand passed over him. A couple of sour looking civilians opened his car's trunk and tossed the only suitcase onto the roadway. Others inspected beneath the hood, the undercarriage, the upholstery and glove compartment.

"Where will you be staying in Pokagon County? And for how long?

Rob was kneeling on the asphalt, stuffing scattered clothing back into the suitcase. "I'll be at a B & B near Lake Maxinkuckee, the nearest town is..." A clipboard was shoved into his hands.

"Fill out the forms, all three pages. When you're finished, we'll take your picture."

After edging slowly along the concrete barriers, he was stopped once more by an armed guard. "You must appear at Pokagon in less than an hour. Present these documents at the county seat, where someone will phone security to say you've arrived. If you're late, we'll start looking for you."

Highway 10 tracked west from Pokagon Village, over a railroad crossing, and then wound through a series of turns on the county highway. At the third, sharp angled turn, Rob slowed to a crawl as he approached the spearmint farm where he and his cousin harvested mint when they were boys. On the gravel path leading to the farmhouse, were two box trucks, dappled dark green and gray. One was a Constitutional Troop Carrier; the other a closed, medium duty, cube van. Soldiers prodded dark skinned families up the steps into the lorry.

Tall maples, painted in autumn crimson, led to Bentley's Bed and Breakfast. It was a sprawling Midwestern country house in a style once popular in the late 19th Century. As Rob wheeled his abused suitcase through the nearly empty parking lot, he paused beside a Ford Mustang. Apparently, Marilyn had already arrived.

Fronted by high banks of white hydrangeas, five wooden steps rose from the lawn to a wide porch encircling the three-story lodge. With each step up, he glanced from side to side until, far to the right, he saw a silver haired woman, reading quietly in a padded wicker lounge. Perhaps she hadn't noticed his arrival, but even with lowered eyes, her lips began to spread into a growing smile. Then she looked up with unmistakable delight.

"Rob."

They fell into each other's arms, holding tight and whispering endearments, just as they did when they were young lovers.

Finally, she leaned back. "Quick, let's get you checked in. Find our rooms. Then, maybe, they won't hassle us for a while."

Lifting his suitcase up onto each step in the long oaken staircase, he glanced ahead to Marilyn. She was carrying his laptop.

She smiled when they reached the second-floor landing. "We're just along this corridor – about halfway down." She paused. "You know, Dear, I asked a bellhop to bring up my bags. How are you doing?"

"Fine. Just a little breathless."

Marilyn nodded while he paused, then strode farther along the hallway. She stopped in front of a door and dug into her purse. "I made sure our rooms were attached, but I've only my own key. See you in a moment."

Once inside, Rob approached the set of double doors. As he inserted his own key, he could hear Marilyn's turning in her lock. Then they were together, kissing, with heart-felt devotion.

"Your bed or mine?'

"I told Eileen we'd call when I found you. Then we can flip a coin."

"Eileen, darling, we're together. Rob looks wonderful, but he's getting old!"

"We're all old, Marilyn. Now listen, you have to do something for me."

"Anything."

"Be careful. You leaving is almost as hard for Rob as it is for you. When you have to go, please don't let his heart break."

"Oh, Eileen, I promise."

Let's Be Tender with Our Resistance Selves Today

by Vivian Faith Prescott

I hold beauty in the landscape of my body,
especially in my arms as I lift this ache of life
to my chest, up near my heart.

I used to save heart-shaped rocks, swished off
the sand and seaweed, brought them home to fill
in the glacier-sauced mud to make a garden path.

The garden is a foraging area for gulls in the
compost and a grave for a baby humpback whale—
her skull watches over the sea, while gathering moss.

The moss gathers a high concentration of this
horrid history, what we're living through,
what we've been breathing in and licking

from our skin, while the rain drums on whale bone
and drips its narrow streams on everything spent.
My narrow view gazes out across this small garden.

I cannot see it all, but I want to see it all, bear witness
to what is beyond my island. It is as winter-worn
as I am now, swept up in a moan of wind and rain

playing deep cello notes through my cabin's eves,
through the ribs of my warm house, through my
callused palms and wayworn feet, a pen set down,
a throat yelled dry.

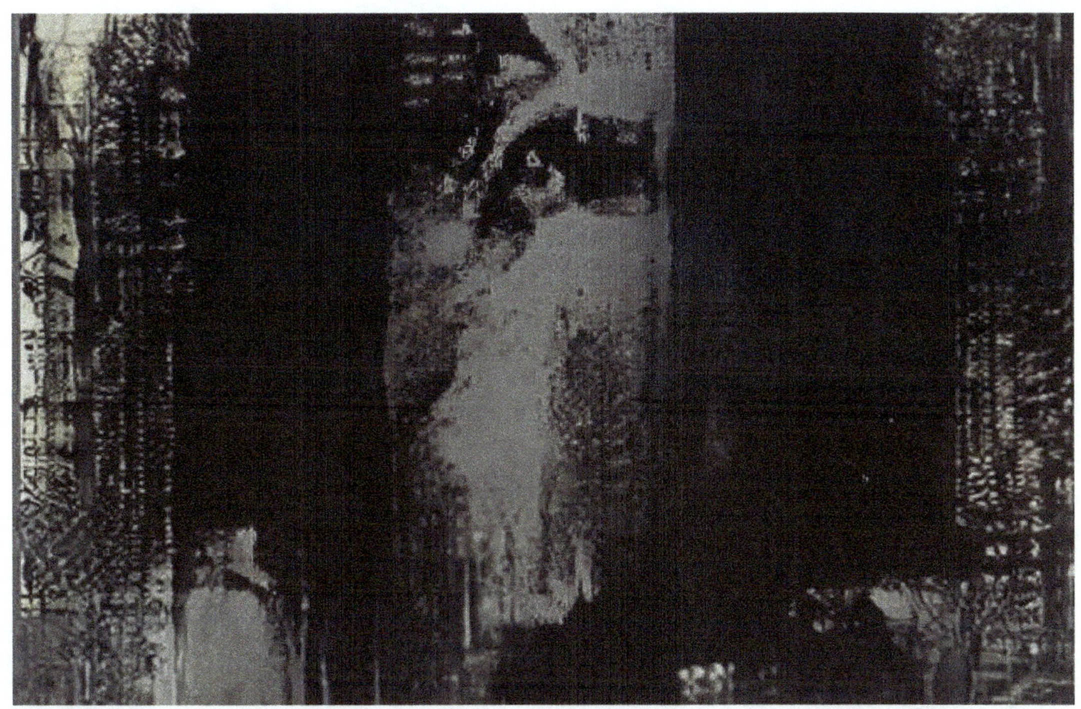

from the series Icons of War

by Tony Brinkley

Talkin' Fascism Blues

by Arika Hendren

The year is 2025
And man, what a time to be alive
Lifesaving technology worn on our wrists
But they still won't release Epstein's list
Many folk think it's right
What we see on TV night after night
Is this a twisted dream?

Well the whole thing started in '17
We couldn't believe what we were seein'
At the time I was abroad
The results looked to be fraud
What's with the outdated system?

Well of the tariffs this was round one
And leaving Paris shocked everyone
We were told to put America first
While the world said, "Do your worst"
From the coop our allies had flown
Into the wolf's den we were thrown
Is this how we end up alone?

Women, feminists took to the street
Across the country in a fleet
In a bid to defeat
The Predator who did cheat
Our system of law.

I came back it was spring '18
Talks of the wall to be built between
Two nations on the same continent
Using bigot reasons to postulate
All in the name of xenophobia.

Then across the world we all did fear
To strict guidelines most did adhere
Seemingly from the East it did appear
Though its origin remained unclear
All interrupted outings, travel and the school year
The world appeared to stop.

Loud ones said all a hoax
But say that to the folks
Whose lives were taken
Whose lives were shaken
All told they were fakin'
A sudden mistrust of science
A defiance for confiance
An utter lack of conscience
For the life of another.

A country torn apart, divided
Information often one-sided
Many a folk misguided
But it came to be quiet
A changing of the guard
Though it incited a riot.

This insurrection
Over the results of an election
Foreshadowed the direction
Our nation would turn.

Trial after trial
Leading to lies and denial
And all the while
A nation on edge
To whom our allegiance pledge?
For politics did drive a wedge
Between family and friends.

What lies next?
For each day does perplex
A fear of the coming days
How long will hate's fire blaze?
For these wrongs who will pay?
The billionaires, surely not they
Nor the corrupt or evil in spirit
Doing their best to clear it
Built on lies and excuses.

Now here we sit
Loyalties split, once close-knit
Future unknown, though it is writ
In the history books subsequent.

Listen To Your Mother, Honey

by Sally Sultzman

Honey, darling, sweet child of mine—

You're wearing that?

No, I'm not criticizing. I'm not! It's just…you're so exposed, honey. Look at your arms and those torn jeans and are sandals—sandals!—the right choice here?

And your face! Your perfect, beautiful face! Do you have any idea how hard I worked on that face? That's right, forty-one weeks. You were late—and perfect.

Don't distract your mother, honey. My point is, you're woefully underdressed for the revolution. Yes, of course I know about it. It was on TV.

You know they're going to be launching smoke bombs and bear spray and—don't give me that look—if you're lucky, that'll be all.

I have an outfit for you. Don't argue, honey. I know global warming has made it warm—it's right there in the name! Give your mother a little credit.

This is not a discussion. You're wearing long sleeves, long pants, and my old combat boots. Tuck everything in. If you're willing to fight for the revolution, you're willing to sweat for it.

The mask is non-negotiable, honey. I cannot believe any child of mine would even think of going to a revolution without a mask! Beyond the chemical warfare, you really want to give away your biometric data? You want them to be able to trace them back to your mother? I swear, you've never listened to a thing I've ever said. I put fresh filters in there. No, I know—it's not "cute." No one goes to the revolution because it's adorable, honey.

Listen to your mother, honey. You can go as a sexy, easily identifiable poster child of the resistance—and not come back—or you can go as an anonymous angel of vengeance that'll leave people wondering for years and then come home to your mother. Which is it that you really, truly want? Because I know my answer.

Good. I'm glad we agree.

Now. Here's a go-bag for you. I've packed a first aid kit, some snacks—you know how you get when your blood sugar drops—a few pints of milk for the chemical warfare, some water, an extendable baton, a stun gun, some knives, and a flashlight. I've also stashed my old armor in there—the carbon fiber stuff you used to play dress-up in. Remember what I taught you—that's right. A forearm shiver is more effective than a punch and does less damage to you. Elbows up, follow through with your shoulder, and make sure they stay down.

No, I'm fine. I'm just so proud of you. Your grandma would've been, too.

Oh, honey—that's sweet, but I'm too old to overthrow anyone anymore. No, I'll be here. When you're done changing the world, come home—bring anyone who needs help, all right? I'll have a big pot of chicken soup going and my tools sterilized. This is only the first day! Revolutioning is hungry work.

But come back home.

Love you too, honey.

That's my girl.

The Good, the Bad and the Ugly Dalit

by Shikhandin

(With a salute to BR Ambedkar)

So far, they have only slipped
in and out of history.

The good Dalit died without fuss.
Without the chopped-up body
parts twitching, drawing
attention to its nakedness.
The good Dalit ate human shit
and was grateful to be allowed
to live. The good Dalit
had her vagina impaled
by upper caste men, again
and again, until she peed and shat
from the same orifice.
The good Dalit was invisible. Kept toilets
clean and man-holes clear.
Did not read or write. Did not question.
Did not break
into protest songs. Did not sport
handlebar moustaches. Or wear
slippers and clean clothes. Or enter
temples and rich men's homes.
The good Dalit knew
that their heads could reach

only the dust beneath
the master-class's toes,
unlike the bad Dalit.

The bad Dalit tried to do
and then not do all of the above.
The bad Dalit protested. Grew
moustaches. Covered their breasts.
Wore slippers and decent clothes.
The bad Dalit
filed cases against her rapists.
Pushed back the toes
of upper-class men, and died
protesting. Worse, her body parts
created scandals. Worse still,
she died worshiping the ugly Dalit.

The ugly Dalit was the one that earned
a PhD and gave speeches
and wrote so much that history
got a splitting headache.
There are busts of that ugly Dalit.
You must concede, it is a human face
and a damn fine one too.
Such nobility, such grace. His intellect
brought disgrace to the master race.
There was nothing for the upper crust
to do but close rank. And sigh
with relief when he died. Momentarily,
they lost the fear.

But the Ugly Dalit lives on. He is
as real as ever. So, the fear's here.
Resurrected. Too true
to remain a ghost. After all
these years, what if
another, just like him, was born
again? Amidst stone fall
and bullet hail, fear lights the lamp.

Fear is the tapeworm suckling
in the belly, swimming,
back-flipping, sunning itself
on the pancreas, oiling its body
with bile. The master race's eyes bulge,
and their ears tighten
with dread. Fear whispers
urgently, "What if
the new ugly Dalit is a woman?"

On Learning the Ten Commandments Are Being Forcibly Displayed in Texas Classrooms

by Jonathan Fletcher

Eight thou-shalt-nots
but not a single command of love.
A prohibition against adultery.
No word on fidelity to self.
There is more than one kind of theft and murder:
stealing from students
the right to be who they are,
murdering the covenant
promised to the ones here from elsewhere.
A warning against misusing
the name of the Lord. No word
of honoring those whose names have changed
by remembering them.
A reminder to rest on the Sabbath.
What of those who can't afford to rest,
busy fighting unjust
commandments about what to teach
and not? A proscription
against worshipping other gods.
No mention, however,
of those who'd make an idol
Of a man.

Instead

by Lisa Meece

There is a vision of the world
    where power is measured in the number of people you're allowed to hurt
        before somebody stops you.
    Competence is measured by the amount of melanin visible in your skin,
    and God's favor is known by the size of your fortune.

This vision is clear, simple,

                                                  wrong.

Ubiquitous.
    But not inevitable.

The cartoon supervillains trying to convince us of this vision
    like Tinkerbell
    Only live on if we believe in them.

We can work for better things instead.

Instead of the pirate code, "Take all you can, give nothing back,"
We can choose Robin Hood,
    Ensuring all members of our community have enough.

Instead of Leviticus, where the wrong tattoo justifies sending people away,
We can choose the Beatitudes,
    showering blessings on the merciful and the peacemakers.

Instead of the evil queen, driven by jealousy to send a child to be murdered in the

woods,
We can choose Snow White,
      walking through the woods and finding friends
      who may not look like us, but who we can care for and be cared for in return.

Instead of Ursula the Sea Witch, who would have us trade our voices for promises
      she has neither the ability nor the desire to keep.
We can choose that kid from the story about the emperor's new clothes,
      Hearing all of the most respected people praising the fabric and tailoring,
      and speaking up to say
      "I do not know what you're talking about, that guy is showing his ass to the
      world."

Instead of Sauron, with his all-seeing eye spreading terror.
We can choose Hobbits.
      knowing that, while we cannot carry each other's burdens,
      we can, when the need arises, sometimes carry each other.

Instead of cowering in fear at the bombast and grandeur of the wizard,
                              (paying no attention to the man behind the curtain).
We can choose the Scooby Gang.
      investigating the forces that make people afraid
      not because we are not scared,
      but because courage and curiosity and connection are stronger than fear.

Instead of the crucifixion, performative cruelty in the name of dominance.
We can choose the resurrection,
      because no matter how bad things become
      there is always hope.
      If we do the work, the world itself can become what we believe.

Ash on the Summit

by Kevin Mack

That magic is greatest, which springs forth unbidden. It was the first rule taught at The Inquisitorium. A rule which spoke to the volatility of the wild magi, be they swamp witches, mountain crones, or the simple village milkmaid who destroyed said village when she learned of her husband's death at the sawmill.

Such events were the impetus to create The Inquisitorium, and it was what led me to the trail of my latest quarry. She stood before me short and slight, clad in the rags of a life lived on the run. An Arcane Enchantress of The Northern Towers would have worn raven feathers and onyx. She'd smell of incense and spell reagents instead of sweat and stall muck. And she'd have posed no danger, for she'd have had the colossally expensive education and training to wield and command the chaotic energy of the aether. She'd have been able to bend that energy into mighty workings of lore and artifice. She'd have commanded outrageous sums for her craft, and she'd have been loved and revered.

Not so this wild mage. She was an engine of destruction rather than creation. Like a herd of plains-runners that must be culled because it isn't a matter of if the herd stampedes, but when. The best eventuality is that it runs off a cliff before it hits a caravan or a city wall.

Such was the danger posed by the wild mage. Her energy builds, day by day, the rising floodwaters that can only be restrained by the dike that is an Inquisitor. And so it would be with this one. I would confront her, press her until fear or anger triggered the release of power, and like a great spillway, I would redirect her destruction back to the tumultuous sea of the cosmic beyond.

I'd been nearly a month on her trail, dispatched to the crater she'd left at the site of her last explosion, picking up the trail that had nearly disappeared in the late winter snow. Then village to village, asking not if she had been spotted, for I knew she wouldn't have been, but tracking the string of burglaries—clothes stolen off the line, or food missing from the larder. Nothing so valuable as to cause much commotion, hence the difficulty in keeping her trail.

But she had to sleep eventually, and the blizzard would drive her to seek shelter. So, I was unsurprised to find her in the barn of the isolated farmstead. I'd hoped the steady gust of the driving snow would muffle my approach, but her guard must have been up, for try as I might, the slightest clink of my armored shoulder against the frame of the door awakened her.

She was on her feet in a flash, knees bent, ready to spring, her hands raised in precursor to spell-casting. But she didn't cast. She met my eyes, searching, imploring. Then she blinked, uttered "let go" and my world up-ended.

A low thrum, then a wave of power—not fast, not forceful—yet it staggered me all the same. She threw me on my back, and then I tumbled the rest of the way to land face-down in the doorway. I was on my knees in an instant, then on my feet in another. I thumbed my spell focus, the charred remnant of a carved horn button worn around my neck, then thrust my palm in a counter-curse.

My spell fizzled. Then nothing. She'd countered my counter.

I hurled a blast. She dodged. I flung an ice patch at her feet to trip her. She dissipated it with a flick of her wrist. She was talented. Wild magi are instinctive casters. They have a reserve of power like any other mage or Inquisitor, but they don't cast by ritual. It only 'happens' in moments of duress or high emotion. Yet her power flowed so easily, as if she weren't even trying to contain it. And if she wasn't trying to contain it, what would happen when she truly unleashed it?

I had to get her under control. Take her power unto myself, then bind her with a Rite of Nullification. But she went on the counteroffensive. There. That blink of her eyes, that utterance, "let go," but this time she didn't throw me off my feet. She threw me into a memory. Ash on the summit of a great frozen mountain. I knew the mountain, and the wild mage I'd found there. Yet this was no memory of mine.

Scilla Birdsong had been a tribeswoman of the southern nomads when raiders set upon her encampment and put her people to slaughter. She would have been the last to be murdered when her power escaped. White-hot and blinding, the fire of her agony consumed the raiders, the bodies of her kinsmen, tents, forges...everything. In its wake, all that remained was ash and wind. Ash and wind and Scilla, alone in her grief, and empty with loss. And now I was Scilla, or so it felt. Living once again, the pain she'd endured. I screamed, her rage become mine, heart aflame, bowels twisted. And in my head, the knowledge that all of those lives were gone, that Scilla was all that remained, and she wanted nothing but to join her people.

She'd carried that pain alone for weeks until I'd found her. Sent on my first mission by The Inquisitorium to trap a wild mage and put her through the Rite of

Nullification, pacifying her power, and her memory with it. Only when I'd nullified her did she drop the button. I'd kept it as a trophy of my first nullification, and used it as my spell focus in the years since. Yet only now that I'd lived her memory did I understand why she'd held on to it, that button that had once secured the cloak of her only child.

Scilla remained in the Sanitarium Inquisitorius, docile and silent. So why was I now caught in her memory? The Rite of Nullification obliterates the power and the memory. It must. Otherwise, the wild mage's power builds again and the cycle of destruction continues. It was as if the wild mage before me had reached beyond the veil between worlds to restore to me that which once belonged to another. Or perhaps…

"Let go."

Before I could reach the answer at which I grasped, she struck again. Fear this time. Licinia Tanica, the youngest daughter of a wealthy but unimportant lord, sent to a cloister for nervousness. The cloister had fallen into a sinkhole, and Licinia had awaited me. She sat atop the mounded earth that then covered the hole, as though we'd had an appointment to meet for an afternoon picnic. And now her fear threatened to swallow me. My hands shook. I hunched over, fists clenched to stop the trembling. I fought to counter it, to guide the power, the memory, the fear, back into nothingness. As I did, I grasped for answers. Still, I found none. Only a thread at which I pulled—The Rite of Nullification binds the power to the memory, then casts both beyond the borders of existence. That I experienced the memory, therefore, implied one of two things: either this mage transcended the veil — Impossible. She'd have ceased to exist. — or that The Rite of Nullification hadn't banished the power and the memory at all. That it persisted despite all I had been taught, all for which I worked…all the women I'd nullified into insensibility.

"Let. Go."

I floated in a vast ocean of pain, fear, anger, and loneliness. Not only those, but grief, rejection, the weight of expectation, and the disappointment of potential unfulfilled. The nullified spirit of every mage I'd hunted, Scilla, Licinia, dozens, perhaps hundreds more. I clawed, flailed, swam through the…what? It wasn't the sea; it wasn't anything, or anywhere. Yet I searched, probed, explored, seeking the edges, a border, a boundary, some kind of reference point. I clutched the button around my neck, as if my spell focus were a lodestone by which to orient myself. I found my bearing and what seemed a wall. Then I followed it. I don't know how long. Nor how far. But gradually I had the sense that the gentle curve of the wall, if that's what it was, transcribed a circle. I understood then that I hadn't built a dike to divert the power of the wild magi. I'd built a dam to contain it. A dam within me. A dam near to bursting.

Softer now, barely a whisper: "Let go."

With a roar and an eruption I was sure would have bored a hole through the planet and blasted the moon apart if it had been overhead, I called forth all the power contained within the memories I had stolen.

I basked in the heat of the purifying inferno, heedless of the chaos I had surely wrought. Windless force beat all around me. I screamed as long as I had breath in my lungs, certain if I inhaled, the super-heated air would incinerate me from within. My voice trailed off into a whimpered nothing and I collapsed to my knees, the power finally spent.

I didn't destroy the world. Or the moon. The barn wasn't even on fire. I felt hands on my face. The mage, eyes closed, a gentle sigh escaping her lips. And in that sigh, all of her power met with mine. In the aftermath, nothing. Not pain or loss. Not agony or fear.

Understanding.

Of her. Not a force of destruction. A force, certainly, but one of healing. Understanding of myself. Not a defender, leastwise not a defender of the downtrodden or the misunderstood. A tool. A pawn in the hands of The Inquisitorium. The keeper of their secret, and the implement of the oppression that secured them in the halls of power.

She opened her eyes, and in them I read the questions unasked. Now that I knew the truth, not only knew it, but had experienced it, would I stand for it? Would I take the reconciliation she had given me and give it to others? Would I fight to end The Inquisitorium and the systematic elimination of her kind? Would I fight to free my fellow Inquisitors from the deception that controlled them? Would I fight against them if they refused to abandon the lie?

I stood, took her hands, and answered, "Let's go."

This Machine

by RJ Huneke

Sometimes I need assurances

by Vivian Faith Prescott

Sometimes, I need assurances
that the sandhills will arrive again, and time
will stretch the horizon across a bleary
gray spring day. You will see this again.

I assure you, the old humpback whale
will return to your bay again, and
the bald eagle couple will sit

in the spruce behind your cabin again.
Sure, these beastly days of beastly ways
are bursting from a pandora-ratty suitcase,

rooting their racist scions into a new
generations' headspace. But trust me—
the fullness of our dark-shadowed

humanity is but a broken-down rusted forklift
in a chapel of thick hemlocks, with a peeling
"America" sticker on its back bumper.

It's not going anywhere. Consider the eagle
shrieking life into this storm, and how the crows
are pecking at the leftovers you've offered

to the beach below. You, go blow the stink off,
a saying your father always said. You can't
outrun this. So go do something, anything.

The politicians and oligarchy regime,
they may want to destroy, but the holy night owl
still hoots—who, who, who—calling you

to speak out, join the resistance even if it's
simply saying, "Damn it, I choose joy."
After all, the owl's voice still pulses

the night alive through the violet dark,
still wing-sweeps through your dreams
with its soft fringe trailing edge—
a plan to persist through another day.

Turkeysaurus II

by Dale Patrick Smrekar

The little dinosaur's official name is Compsognathus, but no one can say that ridiculous name. What's it look like? Imagine the velociraptor from the Jurassic World movies, but smaller, with longer necks and razor-sharp long teeth. At Florida Dino Control, we've nicknamed them "Turkeysaurus." They can grow to the size of a twenty-pound turkey but weigh only about twelve pounds at their largest. They're also adorned in fine, colorful feathers. Lovely until they begin gnawing on you. Then you're praying to God that they stop. Unlike turkeys, they run like cheetahs.

As I drove along the residential road, I watched a young thirty-something man in colorful red, green and yellow bicycle attire try to quicken his pace along a parallel bike path. His efforts were futile. A little adolescent buzzard now maintained a death grip on his calf. "Buzzards," that's the other name nickname we've given the turkeysaurus, because they're always along the side of the roads eating some unfortunate soul. The juvenile turkeysaurus flailed about while gripping the rider's calf in its mouth, its Ken blue feathers flapping about as the bicyclist rode on. They also come in Barbie pink, natural brown with mallard green metallic heads, rust, white and brown. The Barbie pink and Ken blue resulted from early pet breeder efforts to sell them to kids. Pink and blue have become the dominant colors of the species. In those early days after the first turkeysaurus had just escaped from pet breeder pens, the tourists, seeing the pretty little things would run over to get a closer look. Big bloody mistake.

We at Dino Control often found it alarming that parents would frequently sacrifice their kids during turkeysaurus encounters. How could they do such a horrible thing? Abandoning them in the face of multiple mouths full of teeth in an often-futile attempt to save themselves. Sometimes they would even push them toward the pack as they fled. We guessed they figured little Billy or Claire were expendable, because they could always have more kids. But after we raised concerns about this behavior, a meeting was held for Dino Control Officers during which a state biologist explained most bird and mammal parents do the same thing: Leave the little ones behind as they flee. He said it's an evolutionary trait. Some creatures prioritize their own survival over that of their young, especially if they have other surviving offspring to raise. The state biologist made it clear to us that we Florida Dino Control Officers should never disparage parents for making that evolutionary decision.

He wasn't as forgiving for childless tourist groups. He maintained chivalry should command a basic protective action by males among older tour groups. The Titanic story about the men sacrificing themselves to allow the women passengers to board the lifeboats was cited as an appropriate expectation of human behavior. But that never happens for some reason with turkeysaurus encounters. Maybe it's the teeth, but probably it's the screams of the first victims in large tourist groups. Screams always create an everyone-for-themselves mindset, and grandma becomes easy pickings.

Maybe I should also address the *Jurassic Park* fallacy at this point. In every Jurassic Park movie, humans often seem to survive close encounters, even if they have to run from a T-Rex in high heels. They somehow outwit the dumber dinosaurs. After a few years studying the turkeysaurus, scientists have concluded that the typical turkeysaurus is not only cracker-jack smart but getting smarter. In the past year, we've found a decreasing tendency of human survival when targeted by a turkeysaurus hunting party. One would think our governmental leaders would be alarmed by such findings, but human survival no longer seems to be a priority of our state's political leaders. They do, however, continue to advertise their proprietary turkeysaurus mace as the answer to all protection issues, often referencing the success of bear mace out west. Of course, bears don't hunt in packs. But I'm just a Florida Dino Control Officer thinking above his pay grade right now.

Anyway, back to that poor bicyclist. He continues to traverse the bicycle trail, now blocks from where I first saw him, the adolescent turkeysaurus still firmly grasping his calf.

Man, that's gotta hurt, I thought as I watched the life and death struggle of man against beast. I'm certain some of you are yelling, "Just don't sit there. Help that poor guy!"

I had sympathy for both the cyclist and the adolescent turkeysaurus. The cyclist whacked the turkeysaurus multiple times with his bicycle pump as he raced down the sidewalk. His valiant efforts almost caused him to crash into a large street side potted plant. Still, the turkeysaurus held on for dear life. The cyclist soon tossed the bicycle pump. It offered him no advantage. I'm sure at that point that adolescent turkeysaurus was thinking, *I'm bringing this one home to daddy.*

The little blue feathered reptile bounced up and down with each peddle stroke, often slamming into the bike frame or scuffing along the cement sidewalk. Blue feathers spun off everywhere. I became worried for the little critter. The poor turkeysaurus had failed to execute a clean early takedown and now endured a violent thrashing. Every thirty feet or so, a tiny turkeysaurus foot or arm slipped into the spokes, causing the bike rider to shimmy and almost lose control. In desperation, the overzealous creature attempted to set its feet on the concrete to run alongside the cyclist, all the while still firmly gripping the cyclist's calf in its mouth. The reptile's small left foreleg, now bloody and raw, dangled at its side. Still, it showed fine courage, hanging tough and bloodying the calf of his swift cyclist entrée.

"Man, you're gonna take this one home with you, bike rider. It's on you like a permanent tattoo," I muttered to myself.

I kept following the pair. The little reptile's odds still favored its mangling in the spokes or a weary crash into the sidewalk. When they lose their grip and crash to the ground, that's when I swoop in. If they're hunting in packs, it's the next one up. I stay in my vehicle and say a prayer for the rider. Most riders don't last past the third buzzard up. It's always bad news for relatives.

Pack hunting, that's what they're famous for. Just like that movie Jurassic Park, they form flocks or prides. It's an evolutionary trait that improves their hunting success. It's rare to find lone wolf turkeysaurus hunters. That occurs when a male turkeysaurus is forced out of a pride after losing a battle with a new younger turkeysaurus. Those turf battles happen often in Florida. They breed like rabbits, no doubt because of warm temperatures, vast empty lands and a government that protects them. Climate change is the culprit, but we're not allowed to talk about that here in Florida. They've banned the term climate change.

If you've read the internet, you're aware how we got here. The Chinese discovered an almost complete Compsognathus in the ice pack of the North Pole. The Chinese usually start these things - bird flu, COVID, now turkeysaurus. They cloned the first few and watched in awe as they multiplied like rabbits. They weren't supposed to be capable of breeding. That's the story they told the world. The global community suspected they were engineering the damn things as combat weapons. Of course, a few escaped. The Chinese authorities pointed the finger at the local wet market, claiming they were breeding and then selling illegal turkeysaurus legs. Thanks to the turkeysaurus outbreak, that wet market no longer exists. Neither do the vendors. They have enormous appetites, as we've found out. Thanks China!

Within months, an entrepreneurial pet distributor bought a mated pair from some rich Chinese guy and transported them back to Florida. Why? Why not? We've got iguanas, pythons, cane toads, and rhesus monkeys, what's another invasive species in the land of eternal sun. With their cute downy, feathery skin, they seemed the perfect little reptilian pet. Much like the bearded dragon, but larger and prettier. As I've mentioned, they even came in Barbie pink and Ken blue. Enterprising breeders and pet stores promoted the adolescent turkeysaurus as the perfect little reptilian buddy for near teen and teenaged girls. The pets were pricey, ranging from $599 for the plain-colored turkeysaurus to over $1,200 for the Barbie pink or Ken Blue ones. Of course, most little girls wanted the Barbie pink ones. You weren't someone in your local school yard clique unless you owned your own Barbie pink turkeysaurus.

The problem, as most soon found out, was once the turkeysaurus turned one year of age, their dietary needs changed. It became pit-bull time. People soon learned young girl flesh was favored meal of the adolescent turkeysaurus. Even mom made a fine appetizer if the conditions were right. After a few nibbles and chomps, parents would dump them into the wild because no SPCA or animal shelter in their right mind would offer them for adoption.

It didn't take long for the first feral adult turkeysaurus to appear. Where else, but Disney World. They tracked Mickey Mouse down in minutes. It was easy. Disney's character costumes aren't practical when fleeing for one's life. They're cumbersome and the heads jostle too much to sustain a line of sight. It was ugly. You've no doubt seen the video on YouTube. Out of nowhere, three adult turkeysaurus appeared and zeroed in on the Mickey Mouse character. Like most predators, their instincts draw them to the infirm and those unable to defend themselves. Mickey was a natural choice. The video showed them spreading out and coming at Mickey from three directions. It was difficult to watch, maybe because the cameraman was constantly spinning around in search of additional turkeysaurus buzzards.

"I tried my best…to document the attack," the cameraman said in a high-pitched southern drawl to the Channel 9 news reporter after the attack. "I'm just a tourist with a camera phone," he said, his head continuing to swivel around looking for additional turkeysaurus critters. "Visiting Disney World for my very first time… with my buddies over there, Billy Joe and Clyde. Make sure you include them, or they'll be pissed at me." They waved as the news cameraman captured their best toothless grins.

"Good Loooord…we don't have them things up in Tennessee," he exclaimed. "It was terrible... They came from all directions... Man, there was just so much blood. I apologize for the video quality. It was pretty blurry, but shit...I was so scared."

The tourist bystander had captured a shaky, occasionally interrupted scene where turkeysaurus dinos grabbed Mickey's legs and brought him down, while a third buzzard held onto Mickey's flailing arm to prevent him from fending off the turkeysaurus attackers. Once Mickey hit the ground, the two turkeysaurus let go of his legs and lunged at Mickey's face. It was classic turkeysaurus pack hunting behavior. Bring the target to the ground and go for the face. Fortunately, Mickey's fiberglass face held. Obstructed by the large fiberglass face, the dinos searched for other suitable entry ports on Mickey's costume. Mickey flailed away as best he could, screaming and swatting at the turkeysaurus attacking him. At times, his large, white-gloved hands scored a hit, sending a turkeysaurus tumbling away. But sheer numbers left no doubt Mickey was destined to be a turkeysaurus dining extravaganza. That's when an evangelical religious freak dressed as Jesus ran up to the flailing Mickey and shoved a cross in one of the turkeysaurus' faces. The turkeysaurus responded to this new religious opportunity by severing his wrist tendons and blood vessels, then sought other bodily weaknesses. Eyeballs were next.

"Oh no, he's eating Jesus," was heard from the assembling masses in the cameraman's video. A couple of foreign visitors applauded, proving it wasn't such a benign small, small world after all.

To the astonishment of all, Snow White's seven dwarfs entered the scene. The camera man did his best to catch all the action. It was a jumbled mess, as Snow White's dwarfs converged from all angles, creating an epic frenzied battle of superior forces overcoming a smaller force. Two to a turkeysaurus, the dwarfs grabbed each turkeysaurus. Doc, with razor sharp sheet metal clippers in hand, snipped each turkeysaurus head off. Rivers of turkeysaurus blood and feathers flowed everywhere. Once finished, they carried off the carcasses in a large animal carrier to the applause of the many onlookers. There wasn't much Disney's EMT crew could do for Jesus. Wild turkeysaurus are ravenous, like piranhas. They'll strip a bone clean in just a few seconds.

The young girl in Mickey's costume was unharmed, but emotionally spent. "There's no way I'm ever doing a character mockup again," she said tearfully on the local TV channel camera after being released from Disney's ER. "I'm quitting character acting. Did you see all the blood around me? There was an eyeball staring back at me on the ground!" The twenty-something girl trembled, then shook her head and wandered off to the main street ice cream shop to drown her sorrows and recover from her near-death experience.

Meanwhile, Disney public relations tried their best to spin the story. "Our employee is fine. The Jesus character wasn't one of ours. We don't do religious characters at Disney. We extend our deepest sympathies to the family of Jesus guy. While we had nothing to do with the invasion of these little dinosaurs, you can be sure Disney will do right by the family of that poor man. Disney would like to thank our seven Snow White dwarf character actors who rushed to the scene and prevented further injuries to our guests and employees. They showed fine courage while eliminating the threat those creatures posed to everyone. This unfortunate event will necessitate the closing of all Disney World parks for the next three days. We need to conduct a thorough search for any other small dinosaurs that have entered Disney property. Our guest's security is paramount at Disney. Thank you and please proceed toward the exits. Armed security will accompany you."

The Disney complexes and on-site hotels were evacuated in an orderly and calm manner.

News reports celebrated Snow White's dwarfs as heroes until online activists claimed the people dressed up as dwarfs were Disney's turkeysaurus handlers. One conspiracy theory followed another, leading to the unsubstantiated claim that "woke" Disney was raising them for a new attraction and had allowed three to escape their substandard cages. Disney didn't have any of them, but facts never matter anymore.

The following day, a noted television opinion host stated they were cute, harmless, little pets until Disney weaponized them into carnivorous baby killers. He demanded action against Disney. The Florida legislature, being in session, listened to the outcry and rushed to proclaim Compsognathus, the state dinosaur. They also declared them a protected species, just like the Florida panther. You couldn't hunt, possess without a permit, nor kill or injure one without facing felony charges. They even forbid the press from reporting human-turkeysaurus interactions to protect the identities of victims. The governor signed the emergency bill, muttering something about freedom. Florida threatened Disney with massive fines and criminal charges if they even touched another one of the state dinosaurs. Disney World soon closed, having sustained too many character losses.

The pharmaceutical industry, seeing a chance for huge profits, rode to the rescue. They fast tracked a vaccine that enabled people to live alongside the invasive turkeysaurus. The vaccine rendered human flesh very bitter. Test studies showed it was one hundred percent effective.

"Thank God for the pharmaceutical industry," many Florida residents said.

Unfortunately, Florida's Surgeon General, always up for protecting the health and wellbeing of Florida's citizens, responded by declaring, in the absence of any scientific studies, that the turkeysaurus vaccine altered human DNA and demanded the Florida legislature protect its citizens from this dangerous vaccine.

The Florida legislature, never missing an opportunity to promote freedom and pharmaceutical safety, promptly pounced on the pharmaceutical industry, passing the Freedom From Tyranny law, which inadvertently banned all vaccines. It was passed and signed by the governor in a midnight ceremony.

The Florida legislature's swift action was deemed successful and delivered unexpected benefits. Homelessness ceased to be a problem. With no vaccine to protect them, roving bands of turkeysaurus devoured the homeless where they slept. Sometimes when I pulled the graveyard shift, all I would hear were the screams of the homeless. I never hear that anymore.

The turkeysaurus has solved the homeless problem that had confounded local and state leaders and drained valuable tax dollars from more pressing needs. Sure, the snowflake crowd raised objections, but Florida's Surgeon General's persuasive science-based argument that the elimination of the homeless was consistent with the evolution theories expressed by Charles Darwin was difficult to overcome. With more tax dollars available for other needs, the inhumanity of serving up the homeless to roving bands of turkeysaurus became acceptable to the residents of Florida. Funny how humanity prioritizes who lives and who dies. But I'm getting into philosophical territory here and that's not my job. I'm just a Dino Control Officer enforcing the laws of this great state.

The booming turkeysaurus population also cut down on illegal immigration. No migrant in their right mind wanted to live a life running from Turkeysaurus dinos every day. Didn't help Florida's agriculture industry none, but hey, let's be honest, a variety of nations can ship fruits and vegetables into Florida. Seeing the success Florida had with illegal immigration, Texas and Alabama immediately requested Florida ship them some breeding Turkeysaurus pairs to solve their immigration problem. We at Florida's Dino Control responded by trapping and shipping off several breeding pairs to Texas and Alabama. Unfortunately, they arrived in the dead of winter. Texas and Alabama soon found out our small cold-blooded dinosaurs couldn't survive freezing temperatures.

Once the street side homeless population had been eradicated, the turkeysaurus—like coyotes — which ceased to exist in Florida due to the exploding turkeysaurus population, turned to the next easiest to catch nutritional resource, slow-moving seniors. The term active seniors took on a new meaning, as seniors soon replaced the homeless as the turkeysaurus' favorite prey. If they didn't move fast enough, they became menu items. That too had an economic silver lining. The resulting declining numbers of elderly significantly reduced the outlay of funds for senior services, reduced unreimbursed hospital expenses for the elderly and the state's outlay of Medicaid dollars for nursing home care. How the turkeysaurus learned to target nursing homes is a lesson in evolution. Five or six was all that was required to clean out a nursing home and significantly reduce Medicaid expenditures in Florida. It became a win-win situation for balanced budget advocates.

Even Florida's insurance industry liked the little critters. After devastating hurricanes, packs of ravenous turkeysaurus would descend upon the blighted counties, picking off the newly homeless hurricane victims. It is said that Citizens, the state's insurer of last resort, hosted many Dead People Don't File Claims parties, which were well attended by state legislators and public officials. Property insurance rates soon fell, offering a rare win for Florida property owners. The turkeysaurus has helped solve so many of Florida's budgetary and economic problems.

The only ones who didn't like the government's actions were the common everyday citizens of Florida, like the poor cyclist I've been following. They don't matter to our state leaders because they rarely contribute to campaign war chests and thus, are expendable. Our governor saw to it that those possessing generous checkbooks had the necessities of life to enable them to live in harmony with the turkeysaurus. Such as prohibited vaccines, residential security systems, and turkeysaurus trappers to eliminate nuisance turkeysaurus critters. Everything always has a way of working out in Florida

To date, no one knows how many Florida residents have died because of turkeysaurus attacks. The state doesn't release those statistics. Did I mention they breed like rabbits? Yeah, I guess I did. They're everywhere. Today, even venturing to the grocery store can be a life-threatening situation. But it's required, because all the grocery delivery services have ceased to exist. Those services quickly realized they were just feeding the local turkeysaurus population nutritious delivery people rather than filling their customer's refrigerators with delicious food products.

Tourist marketing campaigns highlighting Florida's beautiful beaches have also ended. But it took a while and resulted in many a beachgoer's death. When Florida residents and tourists initially realized the turkeysaurus can't swim, they flocked to the beaches, taking shelter in the water when solitary turkeysaurus critters or packs appeared, giving Florida's residents and tourists a welcome respite from turkeysaurus interactions. Unfortunately, the turkeysaurus soon learned they can wait out beachgoers who, after one or two days treading water as they waited for the turkeysaurus to abandon their beachgoer hunt, would take their chances and flee toward their cars. By then large roving packs had gathered, and when the poor beachgoers sprinted to their car, the dinosaur's long wait was often rewarded with a waterlogged, but none the less delicious human meal. In one case, the trapped folk's relatives showed up and began picking off the small dinosaurs with their AR-15s. A Dino Control Officer promptly arrested them, for as we all know, harming or killing our state dinosaur is a felony.

I must admit, I do wish I had been the Dino Control Officer who showed up on that call. As a result of his actions, the State of Florida was able to seize the vehicles, bank accounts, and homesteads of the ten people he arrested, ultimately leading to a six-figure bonus for him. That property transfer law is in the Florida Statues, and our Conservative Federal Supreme Court has ruled in Florida's favor. Look it up.

Now hopefully, you understand why I didn't rush to help that poor cyclist. That would have been illegal. I'm employed by the Florida Dino Control Division of the Florida Fish & Game Conservation Commission. It's my job to protect our state dinosaurs. Dino Control Officers make a hundred thousand dollars a year and get bonuses based on the number of convictions attained for arrests of people who kill or injure a turkeysaurus.

How'd I get this great paying job? I have to thank my wife. Aileen, for forcing me to change jobs. She became tired of running with the girls between the car and our house when turkeysaurus packs invaded our community. We had been living in a nice, gated community, but that community did not have one of those turkeysaurus restraint systems. Only the seriously wealthy can afford them.

My wife insisted I request a transfer from the Florida Highway Patrol to Dino Control once she learned Dino Control Officers live in Turkeysaurus restraint system communities. As she said during a momentary argument about my future, "You risk your life every day as a Highway Patrol Officer and make what, sixty thousand a year. You should earn far more at Dino Control. The Dino Control job pays one hundred thousand just to begin. My sister-in-law's cousin's husband works for Dino Control. She says, with bonuses, he brings home over two hundred thousand dollars a year. And they live in a dino-proof residential community. Our girls can play outside again."

I had to admit her argument made sense. My wife saw no difference between my risking my life as a Highway Patrol Officer or risking my life as a Dino Control Officer. What I never explained to her is that it's a lot more dangerous. The attrition rate is forty percent for first year Dino Control Officers. No one knows that. The state doesn't release mortality statistics for Dino Control Officers, or anyone else, for that matter. It's all hush-hush. New officers learn fast about the behaviors of Florida's wild turkeysaurus population. If they don't, they rarely survive that first year.

At my initial Dino Control Officer training, they showed us slides of Dino Control Officers who didn't exercise caution and ended up piranha-sized into oblivion. Gross! We also watched a demonstration from a secured building of a poor goat being savagely attacked by a pack of wild turkeysaurus. Unfortunately, our instructor slipped to the ground after tying up the goat and the turkeysaurus almost made quick work of him, too. He recovered but lost the use of his right arm and eye. That training session still causes me nightmares, but it's helped me make it through my first two years on the job.

At this point, you're no doubt asking, how could you work for Florida's Dino Control? Initially, I had my ethical concerns. We all know the state of Florida has prioritized turkeysaurus survival over its citizen's survival. One would think our citizens would have revolted and voted our legislators and government officials out of office. But that didn't happen, because almost no one ever shows up to vote. Not sure why, but I have my suspicions. Polling sites for those who live in unprotected areas always seem to be placed near turkeysaurus nesting grounds, which, along with a ban on vote-by-mail, contributes to our low voting numbers. Landslides elections are common. Once I realized it was the people's will, I dropped my concerns. Besides, my family now lives in a safe environment, in beautiful state paid housing. My precious girls attend the best schools, and we can afford extravagant vacations. I've got a great retirement program, health insurance for my family and a five-million-dollar life insurance policy. You would have taken this deal too. Sure, I'm compromised. But isn't everybody now days. Hell, everyone seems to be on the take. It's the American way. Crap, I gotta go. The turkeysaurus gnawing on the cyclist just slammed to the ground. I need to rescue it.

As the bicyclist roared off, his calf bloodied, but still capable of powering his escape, I drove my truck up on the bike path next to the severely wounded little turkeysaurus. It's a young male. I figured as much. I've never seen a lone female turkeysaurus in hunting mode. It's always the male. The poor thing took a wallop when it hit the cement after a leg had become entangled in the bike spokes. Damn near severed one of its rear legs. The impact with the cement scraped its lower jaw feathers clean. A few teeth littered the ground from the impact zone to where it landed.

Another bicyclist pulled up to the scene as I was pulling on my protective gear and gloves.

"Hey, that's the damn turkeysaurus that's been harassing us bicyclists for the past five days," he said, straddling his fancy racing bike and pointing to the critter. "There aren't too many blue ones around this neck of the woods. That's how I recognize this one. I hit him yesterday with my can of state approved turkeysaurus mace."

"Glad to see you following the mandated security provisions."

"Always. It's expensive as hell, but it's worth it. It allows me to live a normal life. Sort of like those people in Montana with the grizzly bears. Of course, their bear mace is cheap compared to this turkeysaurus mace." He showed me his can of turkeysaurus mace. "Do you think the day will ever come when someone other than the State of Florida can sell turkeysaurus mace?"

"It a big moneymaker. I doubt that'll happen." I replied. "This poor turkeysaurus just got bludgeoned with an air pump by some bike rider. The thing let go after becoming entangled in wheel spokes. It's in pretty awful shape. All so unnecessary. Who rides around without turkeysaurus mace?"

"That's got to be Jerry. He's a real risk-taker. Likes to ride up on a resting turkeysaurus and kick the living shit out of it as he passes by, just to irritate it. Says it shows the damn things who's boss."

"Any idea where I can find Jerry? Assaulting our state dinosaur is a crime in Florida."

"I'd rather not get involved. Jerry's a little whacked if you know what I mean. Got a serious death wish and could get violent. Have a nice day," he said and sat back in his seat, waved and pedaled off. I would have stopped him, but hell, like he said, he didn't want to get involved. I respect that.

I turned my attention to the poor little fellow writhing on the ground. It hissed. Its stubby wings flapped as I approached. They've got stubby little wings. Thank God they can't fly, otherwise they'd be impossible to corral. Can you imagine being dive-bombed by a carnivorous dinosaur? I carefully extended my mouth noose and clamped the little guy's mouth shut. He twisted and squirmed about. Its almost severed leg generated a series of spastic movements, indicating the necessary blood flow and functioning tissue to still receive commands from its brain to flee. I cradled it in a blanket and stroked its head.

"You did a lot of damage, young man," I whispered and then stood up and walked him over to my truck.

We Dino Control Officers receive enough medical training to allow us to administer tranquilizers and painkillers. Two shots and he just laid there in his own nirvana. I placed him in an air-conditioned pen. Yeah, we transport injured turkeysaurus critters in air conditioning. During the summer nowadays it gets in the low hundreds in Florida. The turkeysaurus loves it hot — they're dinosaurs. But when we pick an injured one up, the air-conditioned holding pens in our trucks help calm them and reduce stress. Unfortunately, I'm not sure this one is going to make it. If the docs have to amputate that leg, we can't release it back into the wild. It'll be put down.

I zipped down the road by the bicycle path toward our turkeysaurus ER and noted a commotion ahead. Cars were stopped, people milling about with open car doors looking at the path. As I near, it became clear they were watching a large group of turkeysaurus ripping a victim apart.

"Can you do something?" a lady said as I pulled up. "I think the guy's still alive."

"Not anymore," another stopped driver hollered out his car window. "That's intestines one of those buzzards is running off with."

I bowed my head and said a prayer.

"That's Jerry," a nearby stopped bicyclist said. "A large pack of turkeysaurus were waiting for him. They're smart as hell and when you repeat the same tactics again and again, they learn like crows. There must be a dozen of them feasting on him. Gotta use this turkeysaurus mace when you ride," he said holding up his can of mace, before pedaling off in the opposite direction.

Another happy turkeysaurus ran off with some internal organ, maybe part of a liver, as I watched.

"Jerry, your luck just ran out," I mumbled in disgust.

His stupid move cost me a bonus for a felony collar. All I had to do was bring in a live Jerry. The severity of his injuries didn't matter. As long as he's breathing at the time charges are filed, I'd get my bonus.

"Am I wrong for not caring about Jerry?

legal thoughts

by Maia Justine Storm

when the nazis told the jews to wear
a yellow star, would you have helped them
get one? driven them to the place of distribution?
maybe they asked you for help, not
wanting to break any laws, not wanting to draw
malign attention

when ICE tells the undocumented
to register, to self deport, to pay a fine for their
illegality, are you helping them
fill out the forms, driving them to the airport?
maybe they are asking for help, not
wanting to break any laws, not wanting to draw
malign attention

when desperate clients want an application filed
do you tell them the truth, that
they are only alerting the government to their
address, here i am, come get me
or do you jack up your price, citing serious research
that must be done

pinning that yellow star on a little more securely

Beneath the Rubble

by Kurt Newton

It's where nations have toppled
and nations have been born
to repeat the cycle of destruction.

It's where generations have fought
and generations now lie
buried beneath the dust of memory.

It's where fathers spill their blood
to the gods of the earth
for a promise that remains unfulfilled.

It's where mothers shed their tears
for the violence their mind abhors
but their heart can't help but love.

It's where children go to play
in an imaginary field
under the eye of an everlasting sun.

Tough Darts!

by Adam J. Galanski-De León

We killed the man who privatized water today. We strung him up by his bootstraps above a river, force-feeding him Popeye's biscuits while he watched the water flow beneath him until his mouth dried out, choking. Then from our wells, we drank deep.

The Little Place on the Corner

by Flavian Mark Lupinetti

Many years after the revolution,
we visit the little place on the corner.
She hobbles in assisted by her cane.
I hobble in assisted by her.
"This was the very table," she tells me,
"where we planned it all,
all the while knowing how long the odds."
Today, the only visible acknowledgement
of what happened in this little place
is the corroded metal plaque
beneath the black and white photo
capturing a bulky bald man resting his cigarette
against the saucer, while a thin fellow clutches
a fork with the two functioning fingers
of his good hand. She is between them,
laughing, maybe laughing at them,
maybe laughing with them, it's hard to tell.
"See how tough they look," she says.
"They worked so hard to look tough.
To impress the girls."
"Did it work?" I ask, and this makes
her laugh, but for only a second,
because the words stick in her throat.

"Babies," she says. "We were babies."

Emma's Knives

by Karen Eisenbrey

Dear Emma,

Some would have you believe there's only one good way to make chicken soup. Nonsense. There are as many ways as there are cooks. Here is the method I learned from my grandmother. Over the years, I made it my own. Feel free to do the same.

Invest in a good stockpot. Don't rely on roommates or partners to provide cookware.

Acquire the best knives you can afford. Don't be afraid to use your knives. Keep them sharp.

1. Roast a chicken, free-range if possible. Freedom improves the flavor.

2. Carve off wings, drumsticks, thighs, and breast meat. Serve immediately or set aside for another meal. Leave back meat on carcass.

3. Place carcass and juices in stockpot.

4. Add vegetables. My recipe calls for chunks of carrot and celery in equal amounts, and sliced onion. It is possible to make a satisfying soup with onion and only carrot or only celery if that is your preference. The amount of onion is up to you, but if you will be sharing the soup, it is helpful to agree.

5. Add water to cover, put lid on pot, and place over high heat until boiling. Skim foam or stir it down.

6. Reduce heat, replace lid, and simmer for a few hours. Taste periodically. Trust your senses. You'll know when it's ready.

7. Strain bones and vegetables and allow stock to cool. (Compost bones and veggies, if possible. It's important to give back to the earth.) Chill to allow fat to harden for easy removal, or leave it in if you like; it's your soup

Use in recipes that call for broth or stock, including:

GRANDMA'S CHICKEN SOUP

Chop half an onion (more or less as you prefer). Heat 1 tablespoon oil in a large pan and sauté onion until translucent and yielding. Add diced carrots and/or celery (see above), one cup each if using both. Sauté, stirring occasionally, 5 minutes. Meanwhile, cut up some of that leftover chicken; mix light and dark meat for fullest flavor. Add 8 cups stock (if strong, dilute with water) and chicken. Bring to a boil. Taste and season according to your preference. Soup may be served as is, or add your favorite noodles or dumplings. Recipes available upon request!

Good soup is not complicated, but can take years to master. I hope you find it a worthwhile challenge, and that you find someone to eat it with you who shares your taste in onions. Invest in a good stockpot. Keep your knives sharp.

Love, Grandma

Emma waited for the light, anxious to get out of the sun and out of sight. Traffic — and traffic laws — didn't favor pedestrians. The same people who could afford private vehicles made the laws, or controlled those who did. Jaywalkers didn't stand a chance. It was every man for himself, and heaven help a woman on her own. According to Grandma, she needed to be ready and able to help herself. Make her own soup.

In theory, it was safe to be out. Active fighting had abated to the occasional insurgent uprising, usually in some remote place. Law-abiding citizens with nothing to hide had nothing to worry about. In theory.

Emma gazed up at the tower of the old church across the street. Highrise apartments dwarfed the once-grand edifice. Emma didn't know if they even held services there anymore. That brand of Christianity had long fallen out of favor with the regime.

Would the signal never change? Emma's parents claimed to remember when summers weren't so hot, storms so powerful. Grandma scoffed and said things were better than that when she was young. Emma doubted she'd fondly recall these sweltering days — unless it got worse.

Her long sundress would have been perfect for the weather … except for the high-necked, long-sleeved blouse she wore under it, tucked into jeans, tucked into boots. She'd already sweated through everything. She adjusted her sunglasses and wide-brimmed hat, wishing she could wear short sleeves, like the men at the bus stop in front of the church. Some women did; there wasn't a dress code. Just a

Byzantine collection of unwritten rules that "everybody" knew but you didn't really until you'd broken one.

Was that guy staring at her? She felt self-conscious of her bare hands, but she drew the line at gloves in summer.

The light changed. Emma hurried across and around the church building to the lower level entrance. She tried the door — locked. The directory listed a food pantry, a counseling office, a low-income clinic, and something called Free Range North. Nothing like what she was looking for. But she'd come so far. She pressed the buzzer.

"Who do you seek?"

"Abby?" Emma answered as she'd been instructed.

"Third door on the left."

Clunk. Emma pressed the handle and the door opened. So far, her information was good, but she still didn't know what it meant. She passed the doors for the social service agencies listed on the directory. The sign on the third door read Free Range North — Accurate Bookkeeping, Notary Public. She counted again to be sure, then knocked.

A little panel slid back. "Who's there?" A man's voice, gruff. Nothing like an Abby.

"I'm Emma."

"Well?"

Emma hoped she remembered the correct phrase. "I have ... a gift for Abby."

The panel slid closed. Interview over. Then the door opened. "Inside, quickly."

Emma stepped through. The man was tall, dark, and younger than he sounded. He leaned out and looked up and down the hallway before closing the door. "Did anyone see you?"

"I don't think so." The cramped office was little larger than a broom closet. "Why are you here?"

"Accurate bookkeeping, notary public."

"Uh huh."

"Or did you mean why are we in the basement of a decommissioned church? The rent's affordable and many of our clients are here."

"But why would a bookkeeper need a password and the whole speakeasy routine?"

"All good questions." He sat behind the desk. "Please, sit."

Emma took the chair across from him. If it was a trap, she hadn't yet said anything that could be held against her. To be safe, she slipped a small knife out of her boot and held it in her lap.

"Smart," the man said. "You won't need it here, but smart."

"I keep my knives sharp." Emma didn't care if he understood. She found her grandmother's phrase reassuring. Homely cooking advice and more.

He nodded once, a respectful bow. "Well, since you asked — this is a legitimate bookkeeping firm, for the agencies in the building and a few other clients. And for those with the key, a connection to … something more."

"You're not Abby."

"No, I'm Gabe. Abby's the key."

"I don't believe you."

Gabe smiled. Emma could believe he'd been a student not long ago. "Have you heard of the girl who blew herself up and started the rebellion?"

"My grandmother told me the story." Not her parents. They wanted nothing to do with either side. "That was Abby?"

"She was just a girl, years younger than either of us. I don't know exactly why she did it, but it's clear she'd had it with the powers-that-be."

Emma could relate, even if she didn't plan to blow herself up. Maybe she'd come to the right place, after all.

Gabe's expression turned serious. "If I answer your question about why I'm here, will that help you trust us?"

"It might."

He sat back, gazed at the ceiling, inhaled and exhaled a long breath. "When I was nineteen, I saw my best friend beaten to death by a mob for the crime of holding hands with his boyfriend in public."

"Wow. I'm sorry." Emma had heard similar stories, but not from anyone this close to it. "That isn't even a crime."

"And apparently neither is murder when committed in the name of religious liberty. The killers were charged with disturbing the peace."

"Shit." Women weren't supposed to swear — more unwritten rules — but the word slipped out before Emma could stop it.

"Yeah. I'd guess you have your own story along those lines, or you wouldn't be here."

"Nothing quite as violent as that. Or maybe it is." She sighed. "I was brought up to believe if I worked hard and didn't make trouble, I'd be a valued member of society. But that was a lie. I can't be trusted to make my own decisions, and I was only valued for something I can no longer do."

"It's a harsh place to be a woman."

"We can be harsh right back." She gripped the knife handle. "I raised some money and I want the rebels to have it. I didn't know where to transfer the funds, so it's in cash." Emma pulled a cashbox out of her bag. She released the clasps and lifted the top.

Gabe stared. "This isn't a gift. It's ... an endowment! Where did it come from?"

"Long story."

"I'm not going anywhere."

"Short version: it came from a Wal-Mart voucher."

Gabe whistled. "Maybe my question should be 'how' rather than 'where.'"

"I have ... good investment instincts."

"You don't look like a stockbroker."

She started to smile, then caught herself. "I'm an intern." She wanted to trust Gabe. She didn't even know him, but already she liked him. She didn't have a lot of carrots in her soup these days, and no onions at all.

"An intern."

"You know, get coffee, maintain social media sites, keep your ears open and your mouth shut? Intern."

"At a brokerage? You must have learned plenty. Are they going to hire you permanently?"

"I got the internship so they could show how fair everything is — women aren't restricted in education or hiring. But they wouldn't want to take a chance on someone who's just going to get married and have babies and drop out of the workforce within the next five years. Right? Not their fault women are like that." Something Emma had overheard while keeping her mouth shut. She wasn't about to tell her boss no man would marry a woman who couldn't have children. It wasn't his business, and it might give him ideas.

"Their loss. I still don't get the part about the voucher."

"It was ... compensation. For something I ..." Emma's throat closed around the last word. Lost? No. Something that was taken — stolen. Something of hers they decided she didn't deserve.

Emma had been born at a moment when her parents had paid off their student loans, were both working, and finally had decent insurance. Things went steeply downhill almost immediately — not their fault, but the best they could do was keep their heads down, avoid attention, stay out of trouble, and not get fired.

Emma's own troubles began when she was twenty-one, a full-time student amassing debt of her own. Her fling with Zayden wasn't love, but definitely like, with potential for more. He was smart and passionate, they were young, it was summer ... Then something failed and she had a bun in the oven. No, more like a spaetzle. Her lack of insurance didn't matter. An unmarried woman couldn't get coverage for contraception or maternity care. And she couldn't have married

Zayden if she'd wanted to. By then, he was gone.

Everything seemed designed to make her feel bad about her decision, though the procedure was legal. The anonymous clinic at the industrial edge of a mixed-use zone, housed in a cheap building like the portable classrooms outside an over-enrolled elementary school. The multiple-choice questionnaire with answers that didn't quite fit, with no "none-of-the-above" options. The smug counselor ...

"Do you have any questions?"

"Where is the restroom?" The only non-sarcastic remark Emma could think of.

Counselor Kathy directed her down the hall. Emma hoped to find her period had started and she wouldn't need any services, but no such luck. She looked at herself in the mirror. She could walk away, figure something out. But there wasn't anything else.

"Better?" Kathy's smile didn't reach her eyes.

"Much. So what else do you need to know?"

"You've said you don't plan to marry the father of your child. Does he know ...?"

"No. He died at Snipe's Mountain."

Kathy clucked sympathetically. "We lost a lot of good soldiers there."

Emma nodded. Zayden hadn't told her what he planned to do there, but he wasn't active-duty military. She could easily imagine which side he'd fought on. "I simply can't be pregnant now. They'll kick me out of school if I don't drop out, and I'm nearly finished — one more semester."

"Have you considered adoption? We're connected to a very good home. They have classes right there, and you'd be kept busy until time to deliver. Your baby would go to wonderful, deserving parents."

Emma wanted to scream. Did she look like a high-school girl? "I'm finishing up a business degree. Then I have an internship, and then I need to find work so I can start paying back my loans."

"I see. What are your goals?"

"I'd like to work in banking or finance if I can — use my skills and training to support myself, help other people with their money issues." Use my knives. Keep them sharp.

"What about marriage and family?"

"That's not really a goal." Emma would welcome a family at the right time, but it wasn't something she could make happen alone. "I can't be pregnant right now. It doesn't matter who parents the baby, because this baby ... can't be. I'm already eight weeks along. I need to take care of it now."

Kathy folded her hands on the tabletop. "If you decide to go that route, I'll go over some educational materials with you, so you know all the details of your baby's development and possible harm to your mental and physical health. Then there's a three-day waiting period. So many girls in your situation change their minds when they realize they'll regret it for the rest of their lives. But if you decide to go ahead, the basic termination procedure can be performed for only $1,000."

Emma gulped. That was a lot for her, but she could come up with it somehow. Grandma might lend it to her, or maybe they had an installment plan ...

"... but we would have to add your name to a national database."

So much for her dream of any kind of decent career. Employers always did a background check. "Isn't there any way —?"

"I'm getting to that. With the deluxe package, your records are handled with the utmost confidentiality."

"And how much —?"

"Only $10,000. But ... there is another option. An experimental procedure, but we've had good outcomes."

"What kind of procedure? And how much?"

"There's no cost to you, and you'll benefit a deserving Christian couple desperate to bear a child. Think of it as adoption, but you don't have to be pregnant."

"How?"

"It's a kind of ... transplant. Someone else has the joy of carrying your baby to term. Since there's no termination, you remain anonymous, and the couple will pay for the procedure. It is delicate and time-consuming, but you'll get medical care, transportation, even compensation for your trouble."

It was too good to be true, but once Emma had read the brochure, it sounded like the answer to everything. "All right. I'll do it."

There was no mandatory waiting period. Kathy led Emma through a hidden door and down a staircase to a gleaming medical facility, completely at odds with the aboveground appearance of the clinic.

"We'll admit you now and perform a few tests to make sure you're a good candidate, then match you with a prospective mother. We happen to have a few ladies on site today, so if all goes well, the transplant will be performed tomorrow."

Emma was too dazed to answer. Tomorrow was Friday. She didn't have classes on Friday, so that was all right. By Monday, she'd be her old self again.

The next morning, a doctor visited her room to explain the procedure and have her sign releases. She was given something "to relax her," so she didn't understand half of what he said, but signed anyway. The next thing she knew, she was waking up in the recovery room, her brain still foggy. She tried to sit up and moaned at the intense pain.

A nurse rushed to her bedside. "Don't try to get up yet. You'll tear your sutures."

"Sutures?"

"From the surgery."

There was a word no one had used before. The nurse lifted Emma's gown to check something. A sutured incision cut across her abdomen like a smile — or a frown, from her angle.

"Why ...?"

"Don't you remember? You've had a hysterectomy. Your womb was transplanted into a woman who deserves to bear a child."

"But no one said ... I never ..."

The nurse flicked through her chart. "Is this your signature?"

It was. Emma read something about the "embryo/fetus and its surroundings." Nowhere did it say hysterectomy. She'd heard of uterine transplants in cases where the prospective mother didn't have one of her own, an extreme and nearly miraculous form of fertility treatment. But the donor was usually a relative, or deceased. And the uterus wasn't occupied until after.

"What if I wasn't done with it?"

"You told your counselor you had no plans for marriage or family."

"No, I said it wasn't a goal!"

"Well, perhaps someday you'll be worthy of a transplant yourself. In the meantime, you need to learn how to care for your incision while it heals."

They discharged her the next day, wheeling her through a maze of hallways to an exit that was not the way she'd entered. Unlike the small clinic designed for maximum shame, the state-of-the-art fertility clinic was all about making patients feel virtuous and hopeful. Yet the two were connected underground by an experimental procedure. Emma didn't feel any ill will toward the other woman. She hoped the pregnancy would succeed and the family would be happy. Emma's loss wasn't their fault. But it wasn't hers, either.

Emma left the facility in a cab someone else had paid for (transportation) with a paper sack of pain meds, antibiotics, and a sheet of post-op instructions (medical care), and a $7500 Wal-Mart voucher (compensation). She considered tearing it up, but her good financial sense got in the way. It had value, even if she decided not to spend it herself.

Still in the cab, she sent an urgent text to her grandmother: I need you. The reply arrived before she had unlocked her apartment door: on my way. Grandma arrived ninety minutes later, with groceries. Emma reclined on the couch and spilled her tale while Grandma filled the studio apartment with the healing aromas of comfort food.

"$7500 would buy a lot of necessities."

"If I spend it on myself, they've won. Maybe I could barter it for legal services and sue that clinic."

"It does sound like they're preying on vulnerable women, at both ends of the deal. But even if you find an attorney who'll take that trade, a case like this could turn nasty for you, and there's no guarantee you'll win. And if you do, does that restore your womb, or any other options?"

Emma considered that. She might win a monetary award. The clinic might be thoroughly investigated, or even shut down. But the root cause would remain. "You're right. The real bad guy is a regime that doesn't regard women as adults who can make their own decisions. That's who I should go after."

"You want to sue the government?"

"I want to take them down."

Emma took a week off from school, claiming an emergency appendectomy. A classmate kept her up to date on assignments. She'd have to creep back to school before she was fully recovered, but Grandma promised to stay as long as she was needed. With that lifeline to hold, Emma started trawling barter sites. She didn't want to trade for $7500 worth of something else. She wanted to find someone who needed the voucher more than they needed what they had, even if it was more valuable.

A young widow had inherited her grandparents' furniture. The woman had no space for it, and couldn't afford the storage fees, let alone an appraisal. Her children's need for food and diapers outweighed any sentimental attachment to heirlooms.

Emma contacted her to offer the voucher. When they met the next day at a coffee shop to make the handoff, the mother wept with gratitude and handed over the code to the storage unit.

"There's antiques in there, probably worth a small fortune, but I just can't deal with it right now. Or ever. You're doing me a favor taking them off my hands."

The storage unit was full of solid, well made pieces — tables, chairs, beds, bureaus, armoires, a glass-fronted china cabinet — all in immaculate condition. And in one drawer, Emma found a case full of vintage jewelry. Back on the barter site, she found an appraiser who would value everything for a percentage. After he took a selection of the jewels, Emma traded the rest for a classic car that needed work, with enough left over to secure the services of a good mechanic who was down on his luck. The car went in trade for a dilapidated condo, which Emma flipped for adequate funds to start day-trading.

By this time, she had begun her internship. She heeded her boss's investment advice, though it wasn't meant for her. Between that and her own instincts — and tax laws that favored investment income — she amassed a small fortune in short order. She set up a trust fund for herself — she still had those loans to pay off — but the rest was for the rebels.

"We're lucky our leaders underestimate the abilities of women," Gabe said when Emma had finished her tale. "We'll have to launder the cash through fundraisers, but then we can reinvest it and make use of the earnings. Any restrictions?"

"No guns or bombs."

"How do you feel about propaganda? Winning hearts and minds? Or food and medical supplies are always needed."

"Those would be fine." Emma slid the knife back into her boot and stood.

"May I ask one more thing before you go?"

"Sure, what?"

"Now that we have an endowment, we'll need someone to manage it."

Emma smiled. "I thought you'd never ask. My knives are sharpened and ready."

Dear Emma,

I'm so happy you want the dumpling recipe, too. Small luxuries improve even the best soup. These are rich, but not doughy. The recipe doubles or halves readily, so make them for yourself alone, for you and friend(s), or for an army. This one goes way back, to the 30 Years War.

GRANDMA'S DUMPLINGS

1 cup milk (substitute water in hard times or for lighter dumplings)
½ cup butter, margarine, or chicken fat
½ cup flour
4 eggs

While soup is heating, place milk and butter in a saucepan over medium heat and bring to a boil. Remove from heat and let stand for a few seconds. Add flour all at once and stir until dough pulls away from pan. Let cool slightly. Add eggs one at a time, beating after each addition until smooth.

Dip a soup spoon into boiling soup (this allows the dumpling to release). Scoop up a spoonful of dumpling dough and drop it into the soup. Dip the spoon again and repeat until all dough is used. Cover soup pot and reduce heat to low. Simmer 10 minutes. Dumplings will puff up, so be sure your soup pot has enough room.

(Secret: A different cooking method transforms the same dough into dessert. Bake spoonfuls at 400° F for 30 minutes. When cool, cut open with a sharp knife, hollow out, and fill with whipped cream, pudding, or ice cream. Cream puffs! Because even in wartime — especially in wartime — we deserve something sweet.)

Watchers

by Christopher Woods

now

by Maia Justine Storm

everyone's an enemy now
court clerks, the judges of course,
the immigration officers,
the embassy staff,
ICE cowboys, ICE prosecutors,
asylum adjudicators.
i'm done being polite.

queremos paz,
pero
es la guerra

The Motherhood Plot

by Sally Sultzman

Another contraction rips through me and, as I scream through the pain tearing my body apart, all I can think is—

This isn't supposed to be how things went down.

"Please," I pant after the worst of it passes. "Please!"

"He's breech," someone says, I can't see anything through the sweat and tears and pain as another contraction rips through me, ripping me apart, please!

I'm not supposed to have the sixteenth—sixteenth!—child of billionaire Colm Ffaphington. It was never supposed to get this far!

"The baby's heart rate is dropping!"

"We're losing him!"

"We have to get him out now!"

Another contraction, another scream, I think it was me, why is everyone screaming?

"She hasn't had an epidural!"

No, I'm not allowed to have one. It's in the contract. All natural birth, no drugs. Colm was painfully clear on that.

"We don't have time!"

"Please!" I bellow, this baby tearing me apart, I wasn't supposed to get pregnant, I wasn't supposed to be here, none of this was supposed to happen—

"I'm sorry," someone whispers, the quiet voice somehow the loudest thing in the room and then—

Then they cut his baby out of me, pain slicing through pain, layers of agony I never imagined possible and the last thing I think before I pass out is—

Maybe now I'll have the chance to kill Colm.

The plan had been so simple. Reply to Colm Ffaphington's request for more women to bear his children on his own social media platform, SPQR (Formerly Bleater) using my twin sister's Natalie's profile, get him alone while we were supposedly going to do the deed, inject him with a cocktail of cocaine and enough other drugs to kill a buffalo, and then disappear into the night. Easy.

I spent a few months growing out my hair, living Natalie's life and working on flirting with men. It was for the cause.

That death would've looked natural enough—Colm was somewhat famous for his erratic drug usage and his recent weight loss was rumored to have been the result of Monquempzic, so the mark left by one of those injection pens would've been unremarkable. And if I'd been picked up, I could've said I'd already left after some terrible sex, because I was really pretty sure the sex would've been simply awful.

There was a super-high risk that I would've gotten caught or killed, considering how many guns pictures Colm posted on SPQR, but considering how Colm Freaking Ffaphington had single-handedly destroyed not only one of the most beloved social media sites in the world by turning it into a fascist hellhole but also was trying to do the same to governments around the world, I figured there wasn't a jury alive that would've convicted me.

And it's not like Natalie minded. She was dead.

Killed by her boyfriend, who then killed himself.

That asshole? Also worked for Colm Freaking Ffaphington.

Except my simple, easy plan? That's not how any of it worked out.

The only time I saw Colm was in his lawyer's office. I had the "Monquempzic" injectable pen with me, but the closest I got to him was from across an enormous conference table, where he was surrounded by eight lawyers. Eight! When I tried flirting with Colm, he just stared at me like I was a lab specimen that had gained sentience—but not very much of it.

I hadn't brought a lawyer, only my co-conspirator Jaime Brown, who'd watched enough *Law and Order* to act professional enough to pass as a soulless law school success story. Jamie had donned his finest thrift-store suit and gotten a good haircut from our other co-conspirator, a drag queen named Troya Horse, so he blended in.

So I signed the paperwork while Jamie's leg jumped endlessly under the table. Artificial insemination—no sex, no privacy, no choice in who I saw, where I got care, when and how the baby would be delivered, a cool million upon delivery of a live boy. No chance to off Colm Freaking Ffaphington.

At least, not anytime soon.

I wasn't going to give up, though. Not when multi-billionaires like him were ruining the world.

So yeah, I signed.

Accepting the seventy-five thousand dollar signing bonus felt like a betrayal, but I gave most of it to Jamie to disperse as mutual aid, confident that Colm would hate that.

And then I went and got made pregnant.

"Baby," I slur, trying to push through the fog. "Where's baby?"

"The baby is fine," someone says, not unkindly. "You've lost a lot of blood. We were able to get some anesthesia run, so you should be feeling much better."

The baby. *The* baby? No, that isn't right. That baby is mine. "Need him." I demand, but it comes out more like, "wanim."

A gentle hand brushes my forehead. "I know, dear. I know. But we have to get you sewn back up first, all right? Just relax." Then, "Can we bump her up? Okay, great."

And I slip under the fog and into the darkness.

It's not like I hadn't known this would happen. I was the eleventh woman to sign on to carry one of Colm Ffaphington's "legion" of children, fourteen of them boys, all of them under the age of ten, all of them with ridiculous names like "Maximus" or "Aquila." Seriously, this guy gave the Romans a bad name.

It took seven months for me to fall pregnant with number sixteen, a boy who was to be called Regulus, because of course he was.

At no point during those seven months did I see, talk to, text or bleat at Colm. A woman at his law firm, Matilda Cogsgrove, made weekly in-person check-ins with me to examine my refrigerator, check my "personal health logs," which was where I had agreed to monitor everything from my vitamin intake to how many shits I took, and showed up at every single doctor appointment, but that was it.

Well, that and the guys sitting in unmarked cars outside my apartment—Natalie's apartment—monitoring everyone who came and went.

I was pretty sure the apartment was bugged.

It was a long, lonely few months. But I did get caught up on my anime and completed four freelance projects, so it wasn't all bad.

I stopped carrying around the Monquempzic pen. Because there was no point.

Around month six, I almost bailed. The hormones I injected into myself to increase ovulation were playing havoc with my system, Colm Freaking Ffaphington had bought another election, this time in Uruguay, and the image of that awful man jerking off regularly into a cup so that I could have his jizz shot up into my uterus made me want to get the whole organ removed. What had seemed like a foolproof plan to murder him felt more and more like a trap.

But Jamie took me to dinner, sat me down and said, "If you have his kid, he'll have to come see you, right?" and I wasn't sure I agreed with that, but there was hard proof—photos on SPQR—of him standing next to his most recent baby-mamas, holding his most recent baby (Servius, I think?) trying to look like a happy family, which of course they didn't, but the woman was standing next to him, if I had Colm's baby, I could be standing right next to him, I could jam the Monquempzic pen through his pants, into his hand, onto the back of his neck and it'd be over, I would've saved the world from a billionaire fascist, neither of which things should be allowed to exist separately and especially should not exist together.

So Jamie, in his professional suit and his haircut touched up by Troya again, contacted Colm's lawyers and demanded more money for "emotional pain and suffering" related to the failed IVF so far and it only took a little haggling before the lawyers passed over another check, this one for fifty thousand dollars, because what was fifty grand to a man who makes that every time he blinks? Nothing, that's what.

And that was what I was to Colm Freaking Ffaphington.

Nothing.

That's why I stayed in the game.

He'd never see me coming.

Groggy.

"Dearie? Can you hear me? I have your baby here. He's fine. I'm putting him on your chest to get him to latch on, all right? That's a good girl."

Don't know who's talking, but then there's a weight on my chest, light and warm and someone is messing with my boobs, boobs that are sore, everything is sore?

Oh. Right.

I had a baby.

I *have* a baby.

I didn't want this baby.

This baby wasn't the plan.

Hands move my arms, tucking them around the baby I didn't want but needed to have because…

Oh.

Because of murder.

"Colm?" I mumble, talking through cotton.

"The father isn't here," the same voice says. It's a nice voice. Not the lawyer who's been all up in my business, literally, for months. That's good. "Look, there we are. Can you feel that? A nice, strong, healthy boy. He just didn't want to come out the right way, that's all."

"Jamie?" He'd look out of place here, but I need a friend. And my lawyer. I also want Troya, but I have no idea how she'd get in here.

I just don't want to be alone.

"Who? I'm sorry, dear. The only person here is Matilda Cogsgrove."

Colm's lawyer, the one who's been all up in my business. Still here, in my business.

As if speaking her name had given her permission to talk, Colm's lawyer says, "Congratulations on a successful delivery. I've already authorized the agreed-upon payment to be transferred. As soon as the doctors clear it, I'll be taking the child so you can…recover."

My eyes open to gaze down at the naked little bundle of red skin and wispy hair in my arms, against my skin, latched onto my nipple. What an ugly child. But…

My arms tighten around the baby, my baby.

My bargaining chip.

I worked too hard on him to give him up.

When I'd finally peed on a stick and it'd come up positive, I'd thrown up. Because this was happening and now that it was happening, I realized instantly that I did not want it to happen.

I called Jamie, who came over in his lawyer cosplay. Because Colm's security was monitoring my every movement, we went for a walk down a crowded street and into a coffee shop neither of us had been in before, because we did not have fuck-around-with-rich-people's-coffee money.

"I'm pregnant," I whispered to him from behind the lid of my cup—an herbal tea, coffee was on my forbidden beverage list—my eyes on the extremely large man I'd seen sitting in a car outside my place as he walked through the shop's doors. As if I'd have sex with Jamie in the middle of a coffee shop. "I changed my mind. I don't want to do this anymore."

And Jamie had looked so sad then, so desperately sad as he took my hand and squeezed it and I knew what he was going to say, how he was going to remind me of those photos on SPQR, how this baby was our one and only, best shot at ending Colm Ffaphington for good.

So I'd cut him off and said, "But I'll do it anyway. Just don't expect me to parent this kid afterwards, okay?"

Jamie had looked like he'd wanted to argue—his parents had kicked him out when he'd been a kid, Troya had told me the story once and I wasn't supposed to know—but we all had to sacrifice something to make this work. If I could grow a whole human, he could choke on one scruple.

So he did.

And so did I.

It turns out that, if you refuse to physically unhand your child, no matter what a lawyer says, the hospital won't rip him out of your arms.

At least, the nurse—her name is Betty—refuses to do it. And Jamie gets there a few minutes ahead of several very large men, only one of who I recognize as the guy who's been parked outside my apartment for the last sixteen months, sixteen months that Colm Freaking Ffaphington was supposed to be dead, how did it get this far? Anyway, these three strangers and one kinda stranger definitely would've done the ripping on behalf of Matilda Cogsgrove. Jamie or maybe Betty or maybe both, it doesn't matter, someone gets hospital security in just in time, gets into a very professional sounding argument with Matilda and produces a copy of the agreement I'd signed that clearly outlined I'm supposed to keep the baby for the first month of his life.

Matilda is not happy, but after two hours of wrangling, she finally cedes the field, rounds up Colm's muscle—all of who should be face-punched in public for the rest of their lives—and leaves, but not before getting off a final, "I'll be seeing you soon, Ms. Townsend," shot.

"*Girl*," Jamie whispers, pulling me against his chest, finally sounding as panicked as I've felt the whole time he's been defending me. And this baby I refuse to let go of. "This shit is bananas!"

"They cut me open, Jamie," I sob against his shoulder. "They cut me open without anesthesia, because of Colm."

I did everything that was contractually specified, everything went according to plan—except the baby came early, came fast, tried to come out wrong.

And they cut me open. Without mercy, without hesitation.

I wonder if that's why that witch of a lawyer wanted to take the baby? Because I'm nursing him and now I'm heavily medicated and that breaks the agreement.

I can't break the agreement, not now. Not after everything I've done.

I still have a man to kill.

Jamie presses the Monquempzic pen into my hand.

I hide it against my thigh.

Although it almost cost him his job, Jamie came with me—and Matilda—to every single doctor appointment.

And there were a *lot* of doctor appointments. I was going every two weeks in the first trimester and Jamie and Troya looked it up—normal people only went maybe once a month until they were, like, seven months along?

But by that point, I was going every week, then every other day, peeing into cups constantly, being weighed and measured while the doctor Colm insisted on only talked to Matilda, never to me, and generally being treated like a guinea pig in a science experiment.

God knew I felt like one. The baby—I refused to think of him as Regulus—started to kick and I *wanted* to be excited about it, wanted to feel this little maternal glow, this moment between me and the baby that I was making out of my cells, my blood, my oxygen, my heart—

But it—he—wasn't mine. The legal documents were very clear on that. Colm was the sperm donor and he was paying for everything, down to the extremely fancy water filter that had been installed in "my" apartment, and when this was all said and done, the child would be his.

If I failed, anyways.

I'd come too far not to fail.

Because of the emergency C-section and the sheer brutality of it, two things happen.

One, Betty holds my hand while the doctor explains I'll never be able to have another child. They were only able to preserve part of my uterus—and my ovaries, of course, as if that's a consolation prize. It isn't.

And two? The baby and I have to stay in the hospital for at least another week.

Well, I have to stay. And this baby isn't going anywhere without me. Which is fine. I'm safer in here, where Betty and a small army of nurses and a few dedicated security guards are ready to throw down at any second to keep me from being manhandled.

When Troya Horse shows up, as dressed down as I've ever seen her, I start crying all over again. She rushes in to hug me, whispers, "I know, honey. Just play along," and then loudly proclaims to anyone who stands still long enough to listen that she's my aunt by marriage, and has been so worried about me, but everything's fine now that she's here.

And she stays.

God, I love her.

She's there when Matilda and more muscle come back. Betty, the nurse, runs in after them, already yelling about *visiting hours* and *number of people in a room and family only*.

"She just needs to see Regulus' father," Troya explains calmly, so calmly while patting my hand, she is nailing this aunt thing. "You understand how new mothers are. Her lawyer has explained it all to me and I understand what you think you're doing here, but you've got to have a little grace for the woman who carried this child. She wants what's best for her son, you know?" Troya gives me the most motherly smile I've ever seen. She's so good at this, dressed in her aunt clothes, caring for me, stroking the baby's fuzzy little head as I clutch him to my breast, Betty the nurse standing on the other side of my bed as if she's going to physically block a meathead from ripping the baby off me. "Don't we all need just a bit more grace?"

This woman, to my knowledge, has never set foot in a church, never read a copy of *Chicken Soup for the Drag Queen's Soul*.

But because of Troya, they leave empty handed.

"Oh, sweetie," Betty says, tucking me in while Troya lets out the longest breath ever. "I don't know how you got yourself into this mess, but I'm so glad your aunt is here."

After she leaves, I slide Troya the pen when I hand her the baby. "I think I have a plan," I tell my *aunt*. "We just have to get him here."

"I'll call Jamie." She kisses the baby's head. "You've done so well, sweetie. We're almost there."

It can't have all been for nothing.

We *have* to end Colm Ffaphington

It takes three more days before Colm Freaking Ffaphington bothers to show up in person. For a guy who's paying to create his personal legion of mini-me children, he sure doesn't seem to give a shit about any of them.

Jamie, Troya and Betty, bless her heart, are ready for him. "Two people," Betty insists, with a security guard who's got a whole UFC vibe going on backing her up. "The father and his lawyer. That's it. My new mom is still recovering!"

God bless Betty. I'm going to use some of Colm's cash to buy her a car or something. Or cash. Cash is a nice gift. Everyone loves it.

Matilda argues, but Colm doesn't seem to care. He walks into the room alone, convinced of his own superiority, sure that his special specialness is what has to be passed on—not mine, not Jamie's, not Troya's, when anyone with half a brain could see that we're the ones that have what it takes to survive, to thrive, to get shit done.

"Oh my gosh, hello there, Papa!" Before anyone can react, Troya Horse has thrown her arms around him in a big old family-style hug that traps Colm's arms against his side. "It's so good to finally meet you!"

While she's got him locked in a bear hug, Jamie steps up behind Colm. "So glad you're here in person," he says, and makes a big, manly back-slapping motion, except the Monquempzic pen is in his hand, then it's against Colm's neck, Jamie's saying, "Glad we can leave all that legal stuff in the hallway and just be one big happy family," as the needle goes *click click click*.

"What?" Colm gets out.

Click.

Click.

...click.

It took less than ten seconds.

Colm didn't even look at me.

Anticlimactic, that. But I got him here. That's what matters.

"I am so glad we get to be together for this," Troya whispers, dropping her voice down into its real register, shedding her drag persona like a snake shedding its skin. Jamie pulls the pen away. "This moment is so special. Come, meet your son."

Jamie takes one of Colm's arms and Troya the other and the two of them guide him over to the chair that Troya's been living in for the last week, sit him down, and point his head to me.

His pupils are already blowing out, his hands beginning to spasm.

"I want you to know," I say, "that this was my idea." This little death scene? All mine. "I'd hoped that you would come earlier," like, literally, in a bedroom with no one else around, "but you made me wait and now?"

Now Colm Ffaphington was finally, *finally* paying the price.

"What..." Colm says, but his mouth isn't working quite right, there's a lot of drugs in his system, not as fun as it sounds, is it?

There's so much I want to say, but my apartment was bugged, this room is probably bugged, Matilda could walk in at any second, so I can't tell Colm that he's a bad person, that everyone hates him and no one thinks he's as smart as he thinks he is, that his last name is the most ridiculous collection of letters ever combined in the English language, his followers are mindless, racist sheep with a single, cruel brain cell between them and, most importantly, that his son won't ever be his but mine and he will be raised by a butch lesbian, a trans man and a drag queen, everything Colm Ffaphington tried to erase from this world.

My son will grow up with joy and color and hope and a sense of civic pride and justice and *love*.

And I'm not going to call him Regulus, for fuck's sake. I'm going to call him Nathanial. Nate. After my sister Natalie, who was just one of Colm's many, many victims.

I can't say any of that. So all I say is, "I'm so glad you came. I just know our child will change the world. In fact," I add, cuddling my Nate closer as the worst man alive clutches at his chest, his eyes rolling back into his head, his whole body jerking, "he already has."

And then?

The worst man alive isn't anymore.

Natalie, we did it.

And me, Jamie and Troya all begin to scream. Even baby Nate joins in.

Just like we'd planned.

It was worth it.

Eat Rich

by RJ Huneke

Behind the Veil

by Mark Wyatt

                    Obedient
                servant, one to carry
              water, I wish I could forget
            the water torture. I wish my mind
          were an empty vessel to be filled with
          holy thoughts like rose water. How easy
        life would be! The jasmine-scented gardens
        of my adolescence have deserted me, as have
        the oak-panelled libraries, the musty books I
        read so avidly. I am chattel, a cow, two hens,
      a sheep, my surgeon's fingers at their nimblest
    now, after being broken vengefully with a hammer,
    when darning menfolk's socks. If you can picture a
    woodland on a bright spring morning with splendid
    songbirds flitting in the enchanted rainbow light
    amongst verdant trees, you will know how we were
    at the point when a cloud (full, black, menacing)
    enveloped the sky, spewing ignorance on top of us.
    In dark corners of my memory, there are chambers I
    cannot bear to hear opened, for the screams within,
    for the betrayal of innocence, so that struggling
    to tell this tale now, I falter. Let it be known,
    though, that there was carnage and humiliation,
    with songbirds tarred and feathered, stuffed and
    garbed in petrifying funereal black. I weep when
    I think of it. There followed recriminations:
    suicides, like autumnal leaves, falling freely
    into oblivion; the painful, stubborn silence
    of empty hospital rooms. There is no
    hope, there is no dream, there is
    no prospect of a better life.
    A future bright and clean
    and happy was all that
    we aspired to. That
    hope was snatched
    away from us.

The Girl with the Broken Head

by Shikhandin

The girl
with the broken head
said she would not
play dead. She would
not go away. She would choose
to stay and play again
and again, the broken
record of her war cries.
Even though
she was not waging one,
but only living her life.
Even though they were
nothing more
than ancient songs
of the soil
to which she and hers before her
had belonged. Where
her people had lived
long before theirs.
They arrived
ready to drive
sword sharp rebuttals
and bullet-fast accusations. Recite
their pamphleteered history,
their cinematic deeds.
Their podium-distributed

cultural beliefs. The din
they made drummed out ancient lore,
pulverized to dust
the artefacts of yore. Cracked open
bodies like peanut shells.
She did one thing then. The one
thing she knew to do.
The one thing taught
by her mother
and hers
and hers
and hers
and hers before her...
The girl with the broken head
rose even as she bled, and
spoke with her last breath.

How to Tell a Raven from a Crow

by Benjamin Gorman

to change the subject
we talked about cute babies
and flowers and waterfalls
the turkey chicks led
through his yard by their mama
we similarly followed
to a discussion of corvids
ravens and crows and my local
Eurasian magpies

Audubon Magazine says
"several distinct traits
help set them apart"
such a relief to easily distinguish

between dropping bombs
and snatching away healthcare
between a blitzkrieg and
a reduction in foreign aid
between freezing in a camp in Poland
or suffocating in a camp in Florida

the article admits they
"look similar in some ways"
but no one writes 500 words
about how both have black feathers
a "tiding" of "unkindness"
is a more comfortable description
for a "murder"

Implantation

by M.R. Lehman Wiens

"Thank you for taking the time to meet with me today."

She leaned forward, arms angled outward like the wings of a perching hawk. My implant logged her body language, and golden strands of eagerness began to drip off her, virtual representations of ambition that fell to the floor and pooled at her feet. She looked young, but then, I think most people look young these days. I sat back, reclining into a soft confidence, the fabric of the easy chair whispering under my fingers.

Her crew carried on around us, filling my home office with lights, cameras, all of the artifices needed to make the viewer feel we were having a casual, intimate conversation, make the viewer feel like they were there. I imagined that my husband, in opening the door to our home, had let in millions rather than the dozen or so folks from the production company.

A microphone attached itself to one of my lapels and was quickly joined by a tiny American flag, despite my refusals. Production assistants fussed over me, make-up dabbing over the broken blood vessels on my nose and cheeks. Occasionally a pair of scissors would flit past my face, a sparrow flapping to pluck an errant beard hair for its nest.

My office received the same treatment, spruced up, reshaped, and squeezed into a form that resembled who they wanted me to be. I wasn't unfamiliar with the process of being preened; Emmanuel had a stronger eye for beauty and form than I did, and I was happy to let him fill our home with his vision. He had chosen the haint blue paint on the walls of my office, a dated color from my youth he insisted would ward off dark spirits. That he could still believe in spirits, even in the twilight of the 21st century, was one of the reasons I couldn't help but love him. The dark wood of the suspended shelves, each holding dozens of supple leather tomes, was his doing as well. Even the bindings of my books were intentional; he'd sent my collection off to the binders, covering each one in the same shade of leather, the titles and authors stamped in red felt.

Not that I could read them, though. The implants made sure of that. As far as my eyes could tell, the pages between each cover were blank, rolling hills of creamy white that I was sure still held knowledge, culture, and stories. Each time I opened the pages, smelled the must of paper and the perfume of soft leather, I was disappointed by the emptiness within. Georgie had promised me that the implants were just enhancements, just an opportunity for people to understand, to see more of the world around them. A way to harness technology for good.

Georgie lied.

Even though the books and their titles would be just as censored for anyone else with an implant, the crew began pulling books from the shelves and stuffing others in their place. If they were going to broadcast a slice of my life to the country, each title had to be carefully selected for image and content. I watched them make their choices and tried to identify specific books by their location. The shelf where I stored my nonfiction lost dozens of books, huge chunks of history erased by the censor, while my fiction section was more selectively curated, gaps appearing between books like missing teeth in a rotting mouth. The only shelf not clad in leather, my collection of children's books, was emptied entirely. Colorful tomes of Dahl and Lewis and Lowry and Cleary taken away like lambs. Little indulgences granted to me and my position, but burning offenses in the eye of the camera.

The books that they slid in their place were tacky, covered in bright, glistening dust jackets, blues and oranges and reds emblazoned with the names of party leaders in black. The intruders stood out among the sea of wood and leather, a bevy of the nouveau riche trying and failing to integrate into high society.

The stack of papers on my desk was reshuffled, grown, inflated until documents were spilling out of cabinets and laying in piles on the floor. A worn, ashy tobacco pipe was placed on the table next to me, even though I gave up smoking years ago.

By the time the camera lights snapped on, I felt like a prisoner of time, an old man forced to live within a past he no longer recognizes. In a few minutes of work, they had erased most of the rest of my life, restored me to the man who had once stood blindly at the President's side. She cleared her throat expectantly, waiting for my response.

"Of course. Anything for you, Darla."

She frowned.

"It's Dahlia. Let's try that again, from the top."

Emmanuel was standing in the doorway. He shook his head, exasperated. Of all the observers, he was the only one who knew I wasn't just a forgetful old man. He alone could tell I was being an ass, years of inhaling my midnight breath granting him insight an implant could never detect or communicate. I could smell the gentle disapproval wafting off of him, a sour scent tinged with a sweet humor. It tasted like his lips.

He'd never gotten the implant; folks who looked like Emmanuel hadn't been on Georgie's list of deserving citizens. Even after we'd met and I'd taken him into the circles of power, he'd declined the opportunity. I had pushed hard, tried to convince him of the benefits, both of us red-faced and yelling across the kitchen table, his anger burning beneath my skin with a radiant heat.

There was a time after that when I thought he'd leave me.

"Thank you for taking the time to meet with me today."

"Of course, Dahlia. Anything for you."

She was tempered now, her posture stiff and poised. I'd rocked her a bit, thrown her with my casual inattention.

"Tell us what you remember."

"What I remember?"

I knew what I remembered, but I had no intention of telling her.

I met Georgie in the capital, both of us working as baristas in a coffee shop that oozed bohemian vibes but mostly filled orders for senate staffers. I was the one to train him, teaching him the delicate work of latte art, the Satanic rituals required to get the dishwasher to work properly, the individual quirks and ticks of each regular's order. We were both young then, but where I was a quiet bean pole of a man, he was a dynamo, his personality and movements forming a storm of vicious intensity. From the first, I was attracted to him, drawn to the way his small frame was everywhere at once, and yet still focused on every word you said to him. Through our training, he sank his hooks deeper into my mind, all while deftly ignoring my flirtations.

Our time at the coffee shop was limited, though. Within two weeks, Georgie was fired. He'd been sliding xeroxed screeds into drink carriers, and it didn't take many complaints before the axe fell. I found one in his locker after he left, a black and white sheet, the printer ink fading and running out towards the bottom. Long, rambling paragraphs about the need for society to seize power from the secret elites, the liberation hiding within technology, and the dangers of unconventional living. Much of the language I read was softened, hidden behind euphemisms like "preservation of national identity." Years later, I heard a rumor that the paper that got him canned had been more explicit, quotes from *The Protocols of the Elders of Zion* printed in Georgie's scrawling hand.

"I didn't waste your time, did I?"

He was waiting behind the shop when my shift ended at 11 AM, sitting on top of the dumpster and pulling hard on a neon blue vape pen. I had opened that morning and was looking forward to going home, taking a nap on the couch, and then exchanging my tip money for some green at a dispensary. God, I miss legal weed.

"No, you didn't waste my time. It's a coffee shop, people come and people go." Somehow, I was still willing to be polite, still willing to engage someone that spoke to me with a smile.

"Good. I'm glad." He exhaled, and a burst of blueberry smoke floated past me into the street.

"Can't say I've ever seen someone get fired like that, though."

He laughed.

"Yeah, well, I figured I had to punch holes in the dam somehow. We've got to make people realize that the people in power aren't really in power. We have to go deeper, pull back the curtain on who's really running things, and excise the rot from the roots. The world hasn't worked for people like you and me in years, all because of them," he said, raising his eyebrows. It wasn't necessary. I knew what he was getting at.

"Oh, come on. You can't actually believe all that conspiracy nonsense?"

He shrugged.

"The real conspiracy is believing that people like us still have a chance in this world. It may be unpopular, but I have the truth. I'm going to speak it wherever I'm at, and hope people have ears to hear it. Once I finish my degree, I'll retire the pamphlets and dive straight into the currents of power."

His evasiveness annoyed me, but I still didn't leave. There was an invitation in his words, an open hand asking me to hear him out. He wanted to talk about his tracts, his ideas. Even as a naif, young, not yet implanted, the danger hiding behind them was clear. But still, we were having a conversation. Stuck between the rudeness of confrontation and thorns of his ideology, I sidestepped.

"What are you getting your degree in?" I asked, pretty sure I knew. Back then, any young white guy you met in the capital, it was geopolitics. Poli-sci. Communications. How to be an insufferable blowhard by the time you're twenty-five.

"English Lit."

"Yeah?" I said, trying not to let my tone say what I'm sure he already heard a thousand times.

In this economy? What do you even do with that degree?

"Yup," he said, pulling long and hard on his vape. "It's the study–" he exhaled, an undeniably theatrical gesture, "—of the human mind. Of history. Of culture."

"And that will take you closer to power?"

"You think it won't? They want you to think the future is inevitable, that all we have to do is let liberalism run the show and everything will be okay. I refuse to be complacent, Mike. The future is coming, Mike, and I'm going to make it work for all of us. An implant in every man, woman and child."

At that time, implantation was nascent, more of a dream in the bowels of tech websites. In the two weeks Georgie had worked at the coffee shop, I'd heard him mention it enough times that I'd researched it myself, scrawling through comment threads that promised everything from unlimited knowledge to brain control.

"Isn't that dangerous, though? So much untested technology, so many people?"

"Maybe. I tend to view it as empowering. Or at least, it will be for those of us who know what to do with it." His eyes glinted, powerful, intoxicating. "I'm not talking about giving people all the knowledge of the world; that you have to earn. But imagine an implant that can enhance your understanding of emotions, relationships, bond you to other implantees and give you the insight to work as one. Something to give us an advantage. If they want to rig the game, we have to rig it right back." I remember wondering if his vape wasn't something stronger, if the smoke he was blowing wasn't catching and pooling in my mind. I could hear the promise in his voice, the opportunity to escape the inevitable.

"And you think that will change things?"

"If the world won't work for us, we have to make it into something that will. Do you think we have any other choice?"

My answer surprised me, leaping off my tongue as if it had been waiting for a cue.

"I don't know."

He nodded, pleased. Then, in one graceful movement, he leapt off the dumpster, landing inches from me. I tried to step back, and hit the wall of the alley. Beneath the fruity scent of his vape, he smelled like ashes and Dove soap.

"That's all I ask, Michael Miller. If you can admit you don't know, all paths lay open."

When he left the alley, I followed him.

Little flames danced behind her eyes, cold fury that made her smile all the more chilling.

"Yes, tell us what you remember of Freedom Day."

"You mean the election?"

She nodded.

"I always thought Freedom Day was a funny thing to call it."

She ignored my barb. Her eyebrows pushed upward, prompting me to continue.

"Oh, let's see. George Stacey, everyone called him Senator Georgie back then, was fired up. There wasn't a clear winner, the vote split between the two Georgie and the two old men. He spent all night on the phone kissing ass with any member of the House that would take his call. I sat with him, listening as he went through the slogans, an implant for every man, woman, and child, power to the people, take our country back. Occasionally, he'd go quiet, and then he'd change the subject, ask about a representative's family. Mind you, there hadn't been any violence, at least not on Georgie's orders, but the undertones of his questions were clear.

"He thought we were on the right side of things, but then, I suppose we all did. Magic of hindsight. We were scared, and it seemed like letting Georgie have his way was the only way forward," I continued, shrugging.

The cameraman gasped slightly, taken aback by my blatant subversion. Two producers glanced at each other and began to whisper in the corner, scandalized, secretive.

"When the vote came down, there wasn't any celebrating. Even as the new Vice President, I couldn't find the energy to be excited. I think that surprised him. That's why all the history books say that we broke out in cheers. Can't have that kind of implication hanging over President Stacey and his dawn of freedom."

"What implication?"

"That when we finally got what we wanted, what Georgie had been leading the country to, we were scared. All that work, all those speeches and marches and righteous anger...we'd bought the gun, loaded it with bullets, and now there was nothing left but to pull the trigger."

Dahlia sat back, annoyed, and my implant traced blue currents of electricity across her scalp.

"The implantations went out to his supporters, and then the Reform Bills began. You know the rest," I finished, tapping the flag on my lapel. The red and white stripes glinted in the light, and the single eye winked on its field of blue.

"Getting back to the topic at hand," she paused, checking her notes, giving editors a space to cut my monologue, "this week marks forty years since Freedom Day. How do you think you and the other Freedom Fathers will be remembered?"

"I think we'll be remembered how we deserve to be remembered."

"I'm sorry about Emmanuel," Georgie said from the holopad on my desk.

Emmanuel had been harassed on the street by a group of Georgie's goons that afternoon, a pack of hyenas that didn't care how close Emmanuel was to the nexus of power, only that he was brown, and gay, and present. They were in town for the vote, hyped up and emboldened in the wake of the Reform Bill passing the House that morning.

I didn't ask Georgie how he knew what had happened to Emmanuel.

"Thank you, Mr. President."

"You're welcome," he said brusquely, disposing of the formality with barely disguised disgust. "Why are you calling?"

"What about it?"

He didn't beat around the bush.

"I need you to step down."

My breath came up short, a gasp pulled through the decayed stench of a burial shroud.

"Michael?"

"What the fuck, Georgie?"

He turned bright red. No one called him Georgie anymore.

"Michael, I can't have a–" his lips pursed together, dancing around the letter F, and then his face relaxed "--a gay man as a vice president. Not with the changes we put in the Reform Bill. Not with the direction the people want us to go."

"Oh, fuck off about the people. I'm one of the people, Georgie. You said it wouldn't be an issue, over and over. When I joined the campaign, all that talk about gay rights and–

"Goddamnit!" He exploded, audio distortions crackling around the edges of his scream. "This isn't your decision to make, Mike. I said you're out, and you're out."

As soon as the holopad switched off, I turned to my computer and began writing. My implant picked up on my distress, and each floated up before my eyes, inky lines that vined together in a swirling, vicious ouroboros. I was angry, I was hurt, but most of all, I was embarrassed. All this time I'd thought I was immune, thought that I could be a voice of moderation in the administration. I'd been stupid, but no more.

The letter complete, I pasted it into the body of an email and hit send. I imagined the phones of news editors across the country lighting up, my warning burning through the presses. And then I went home and prepared for the worst.

Emmanuel and I spent that night waiting for a pounding on the door, to be blinded by bright points of light on the ends of guns, stars to guide us out to a waiting van. For the first time in weeks, we slept in the same bed, all our arguments about the implants and Georgie and his agenda forgotten. Fully clothed, we held each other's hands, occasionally drifting off, but never for very long. As the first rays of sunlight crept into our bedroom, it felt as if a great breath had been released, the night finally moving aside to let us inhale, even if for a moment.

My letter was never published, though. Instead, a push notification on my phone informed me that I had stepped down for health reasons and was being replaced by the Secretary of State. By the end of the week, my replacement stood next to Georgie as he proudly signed the Reform Bill.

That evening, Emmanuel turned out his lamp and pulled himself close to me, his head resting on my chest. I reached to my bedside table, my fingers tracing the edge of my bookmark. I can't remember now what I was reading, but I know it was a comfort read, the spine soft and flexible after many journeys through the pages. Exactly what the day called for. When we first met, we often fell asleep in that position; Emmanuel's head rising and falling with my breath, his eyes closed, content to sleep in the warm light of my lamp.

That night, though, when I opened the book, I saw nothing but blank pages. It is seared in my memory, the dysphoria, the loss, the words catching on the paper for just a moment before the implant caught up and erased them. Emmanuel woke to my cries, to me storming through the house, pulling book after book off my shelves, clawing at my eyes, cursing, raging.

It took hours for me to calm down, waves of misery punctuated only by the busy signal on Georgie's private line. He never reached out, never returned my calls. For a few days, I had dared to think that he had let me live out of some sense of mercy, or perhaps loyalty. In that moment, though, I felt his malice. This was my punishment; where others with the implants see only what he allows, I am allowed to see nothing. Nothing but the end of all the worlds I held dear.

Finally, tired and spent, I let Emmanuel take me back to our room. He picked up my book from the floor where I'd tossed it, smoothing the bent pages, the broken spine. Then, he pulled me into bed and began to read. His words have rocked me to sleep every night since then, and in the softness of his voice, I can hear his forgiveness.

She was beginning to catch on, starting to realize that I'd never give her quite the soundbite she wanted. Her eyes narrowed slightly, focusing down on me. Her skin shivered before me, serpent scales moving down her arms like ripples on a lake. She snapped at the producer, and the room cleared. I could feel the click of the door latch on my teeth, sharp and honest.

"Vice President Miller, you've been left to your own devices for years." She nodded to the door. Emmanuel had retreated to our bedroom, but Dahlia and I both knew what she meant.

"That kind of...how shall I say this? Anonymity? Privilege? Comes at a price. President Stacey expects that you'll deliver a very specific message for him, one where you toe the line."

"And now the mask comes off," I said, leaning forward.

She raised her eyebrows, and smirked. It was an expression I hadn't seen in years: disdain. Pity, even. My implant rendered it as a graying that rolled across the room like oily smoke and licked at my collar.

"Mr. Vice President, if you needed the mask to come off, you're out of practice. You know as well as I do what this is."

Her eyes flashed, and I suddenly felt a presence in my mind, pulsing just behind my jaw.

"You're implanted."

"Of course," she said, her bared teeth sharpening into virtual daggers. "In fact, I'm insulted that you thought I was some lackey you could push around," she continued. "Now, drop the confused old man routine, give me what I need, and you'll be left to whatever...aberrations...fill your time these days."

I leaned back into my chair, straightening the tie that Emmanuel had insisted I wear. She smiled.

"No need to be embarrassed, Mr. Vice President. We all learn our place in society sooner or later." She stood, straightening her dress, and moved to the office door.

"Wait."

She hesitated, her hand on the doorknob.

"Why bother with me at all?"

Her smile was full of putrescence, bile and rot spilling down her chin.

"Because Georgie knows you'll do it. He enjoys watching you submit."

And then she opened the door, and let her crew back in.

As they entered the room, I did what I should have done from the start, reaching out to them with my mind, feeling for receptors. None of them were implanted, their eyes dull and biological underneath my probing.

She looked at me, and nodded.

"Are you rolling?"

"Rolling," a producer echoed.

"On this Fortieth Freedom Day, I think of the brave souls who led the charge into the new world and made implants a gift to all people. President George Stacey, you have my mind, my soul, my heart. Hail the Fathers of Freedom."

And then, they disappeared. Dahlia stepped out almost immediately, hissing something poisonously inaudible at one of the producers. In minutes, the light rigs came down, the cameras were packed away, and I was left alone in the ruins of my office. They didn't bother to clean up after themselves, or even to take their props with them. As I looked at my bookshelves, now filled with propaganda pieces by Georgie and his lackeys, I couldn't help but think that was the point.

"I don't know why you have to push them like that," Emmanuel said as he stepped into the room. "It's bad enough that you insist on keeping all these books out in the open. I know you can't read them, but me and every other unimplanted peon knows you're crossing a line." He moved to the desk and began moving prop pages of gibberish from my desk to the recycling bin.

"They don't come around that often," I said, trying to hide the defeat in my voice. "Besides, none of that will make it on air. They'll edit down what they need and burn the rest. That's what they always do."

"I just don't think we should poke a sleeping bear, Michael. If they leave us alone, can't we just give them what they want?"

I knew what Emmanuel wanted. I knew he wanted us to die in each other's arms, to fall asleep each night between now and then safe and together. He wanted to keep reading to me each night, moving our way through the blank pages together. It would be so easy to do.

Georgie stared up at me from the back of his autobiography; age had been less kind to him than it had to me. His hair was completely gone, and his watery lips were framed by jowls that would put a bloodhound to shame. His eyes were still the same, though. Even in a photo, I could feel that bright blue charisma threatening to boil off the page, burning my hands as it flowed up my arms to my heart.

He used to look at me in a way no other man ever has, not even Emmanuel, and I would feel my chest swell. I never knew what he wanted until the moment he said it, but as soon as the words left his mouth it always seemed to make sense to me. Within his words I found the thunder of every orgasm, the fire of every singular joy, until suddenly I looked at my hands and could not contemplate what I'd done. I could love Emmanuel for a thousand years and still feel the red stains on the tips of my fingers. I will never tell him this, but there is no amount of love he can give me to still the guilt from rotting my soul. I never pulled any triggers, but if you put a gun in someone's hand, aren't you responsible for what they do with it? Emmanuel has forgiven me, and it isn't enough.

I opened the hall closet and dumped the pile of propaganda on the floor. I hate to keep them around, to even look at them, but fuel for the woodstove always runs short, even in our warming winters. As I picked through the stack of books they'd removed from my shelf, it seemed smaller than I remembered. I wasn't surprised; it's happened before, each time that people from outside step into my office. This time, though, the number of books missing hit me in the stomach, hard enough that I inhaled sharply through my teeth. Something was changing.

Watching Emmanuel place them back on the shelf, I reveled in the little gaps that remained where books had once stood. Taking a few steps back, I let the fullness of the floor to ceiling bookshelf fill my view. I wished I could talk to each person who had taken a book, ask them what they were taking, let them know what I thought about it, invite them over for tea when they were done. Another joy that Georgie has taken from me.

Emmanuel's blue-painted wall peaked through the books, little slots of sky amidst the dark wood and leathered books. The shelf of children's books remained empty. The rest of my shelves were full of gaps, places where people, a cameraman, a producer, an intern, considered a question and admitted they didn't know. Places where they weighed their fear against their curiosity, and chose the latter. Each of them free of an implant, free to read, to see. Free to act. Free to punch holes in the dam.

How It Begins

by Myles Gordon

My mother watched me
make papier-mâché worlds
from newspaper strips

soaked in flour and water
wrapped around
an inflated balloon

dried, hardened,
a melon-sized oval
the texture

of a hornets' nest.
Already stung by the hornets
infesting the center of the world,

my mother
smoked cigarettes
looking out the kitchen window.

I rubbed the wet brush
on the button-shaped colors
painting over the flaky

headlines and newsprint
in my version
of the world's colors and shapes:

square house,
stick figure family,
my mother expressionless with

the two black dot eyes
and flat red mouth
I could manage at six.

Rather than look at my world
she stared out the window
at her own that she fled at six

(how could I even
comprehend it) Poland,
Brest Litovsk, 1933

local work shirt
thugs with clubs
widening paths

for the coming Nazis
who carried off
her mutilated grandparents

aunts, uncles, cousins
to feed the larvae
of the master race.

Today, in America, face-masked ICE is kicking in
grandparents' doors, rounding up
factory workers from the auto plant,

farm workers from the harvest,
students as they leave
apartments or compact cars

to hurry to class, and stuffing them in
complicit prisons. National
Guard troops

with automatic weapons
infest cities like locusts
in green and beige fatigues.

Scared children peek from windows.
Husbands and wives
whisper into the night.

No one sleeps.
This is how it begins
I imagine my mother saying

even though she hardly ever speaks,
cigarette smoke forming
grey curtain over white curtain.

I remember sometimes
I would crush
the papier-mâché —

ripping and squeezing
shards as if from a hollow
hatched egg.

Someone is always
tearing the world apart
with nothing but malevolent bare hands.

Refugees

by Leah Mueller

(for Basel Adra)

Each morning, he awakens
to the same gunfire, the same pain.

He sees the enemy's
implacable face: square body
bundled into a gray flak vest,
weapon clutched inside an outstretched glove.
His home once more reduced to rubble.

He moves his possessions
to a different structure,
and then to another, each
more remedial than the last.

Water is scarce, food almost nonexistent.
Loaf of bread, spoonful of white rice.
Sometimes, a few vegetables.

The young eat first.
Parents devour whatever remains.

Elders know when airstrikes are coming,
sense the impact deep within their bones.
Still, they laugh. They nap. They play with the children.

They cover their wounds with strips of cloth.

Each afternoon, he hits the road:
trudging through dust, demanding freedom
that he may never live to see.
Townspeople cluster around him, chanting
as they clutch handmade signs.

Their slogans dream of a home
where Palestinians belong at last—
a land that lies right in front of them,
and yet seems as distant as sleep.

let us be dandelions

by Adam C. Lipscomb

blooming in cracked sidewalks
roots deep and hard to pull
stubborn and beautiful

casting seeds of resistance
far and wide
on every gust of wind

from the series Icons of War

by Tony Brinkley

Feel the bones of your knuckles

by R.J. Huneke

Feel the bones of your knuckles
And close your fist
Resist!
Resist!
Smooth, yet sharp, your fist
Powerful with a surety
Beyond all bullies

Trust has to be earned
Well, so does fear
Make them fear
It has been earned
Make them fear;
Inevitable is this:
All fascists fall.

Invocations

by Joanna Michal Hoyt

I see what you are doing. This is wrong.
I'll tell the world. People won't stand for this.

*****

Hold on! You can't arrest me for free speech.
My First Amendment rights....

        ...I plead the Fifth.

...Remember, please, the Eighth...

*****

You have the power to deny my rights,
But you are wrong, and history will judge you.

*****

It seems you are rewriting history.
But whether anybody knows or not,
I still say this, believe this, stand by this:
Far better to be me, and in your power,
Than to be you and do what you are doing.

*****

Well, God forgive me, we are not so different.
I know what I wish I could do to you.
Thank God I can't. I hope that if I could
I'd still choose not to. But I'd have to choose.
You could choose, too, my brother.
You...
I...
We...

*****

When all the human words run dry,
Recall the words the angels said
Each time that they appeared to humankind:
Be not afraid.
Be not afraid.

I read that perfect love drives out all fear.
I don't know how to love like that.
And yet...
            and yet....

Be not afraid.

Be not afraid.

Be not afraid.

About the Authors

Maia Justine Storm is a 77-year- old woman living in Kalamazoo. Michigan with an Amazon parrot and a cat here and there. She has been an immigration attorney for 25 years but has finally returned to her adolescent dream of being a poet. The Poetry Super Highway has chosen her as a Poet of the Week.

Carrie Schweiger lives in the Pacific Northwest with her husband and her daughter. By day, she investigate how magic smoke escapes from electronic circuits and dreams of magical places and people by night. She love to knit, travel, and learn new languages when she's not writing. She's a member of the Historical Novel Society, Society of Children's Book Writers and Illustrators, and Pacific Northwest Writer's Association.

Allan Lake, originally from Saskatchewan, has lived in Vancouver, Cape Breton Island, Ibiza, Tasmania and Melbourne. Lake won Lost Tower Publications (UK) Competition 2017 and Melbourne Spoken Word Poetry Fest/The Dan 2018. Poetry Collection: *Sand in the Sole* (Xlibris, 2014). Poetry Chapbook (Ginninderra Press, 2020): *My Photos of Sicily*.

Flavian Mark Lupinetti a poet, fiction writer, and heart surgeon, is the author of *The Pronunciation Part* (2025), winner of the The Poetry Box Chapbook Contest. Mark's work has appeared in *Barrelhouse, Cutthroat, december, Redivider, ZYZZYVA,* and elsewhere. A West Virginia native, Mark lives in New Mexico.

Amanda Cherry is a Seattle-area queer, disabled nerd who still can't believe people pay her to write stories. In addition to her novels, she's the author of TTRPGs, screenplays, and short fiction, and a cast member in the Dungeon Scrawlers GREYMANTLE game on Twitch. Her nonfiction writing has been featured on ToscheStation.net, ElevenThirtyEight.com, and StarTrek.com. Amanda is a member of SAG-AFTRA, SFWA, & Broad Universe. Follow Amanda's geekery on Twitter & TikTok @MandaTheGinger or visit
 www.thegingervillain.com

Beulah Vega is a Mixt-Latine horror writer, political poet, and (overworked) theatrical artist living and working in California's Bay Area. Her poetry has most recently been published in *Writer's Resist, La Raiz Magazine, Trashlight Press,* and *Blood and Bourbon,* among others. Her poem *Cyclical* is nominated for the Best of the Net 2025 through *Sage Cigarettes*. She is interested in work that gives voice to those traditionally marginalized in the arts. She is still amazed when people refer to her as a writer, every time. www.bfvegaauthor.com

Andrés Castro, a PEN member, is listed in *Poets & Writers Directory*, and keeps a personal blog, *The Practicing Poet*. His poetry appears in the anthologies *America's Slide Towards Authoritarianism*, *Off the Cuffs: Poetry by and About the Police*, and *We Are Antifa*; and as well as in the pedagogical text *Teacher Agency for Equity*. Online publications such as *Counterpunch*, *Montreal Serai*, *New Verse News*, and *Kweli* have included his poems, essays, and short stories. Andrés is currently looking for supportive volunteers, submissions, and donations for the fledgling project, www.militanthumanist.org.

Tony Brinkley taught literature at the University of Maine. He is the author of *Stalin's Eyes* (Puckbrush Press), *Gomorrah* (Cerise Press), and the editor (with Keith Hanley) of *Romantic Revisions* (Cambridge University Press). His poetry and translations have appeared in *Mississippi Review*, *Another Chicago Magazine*, *Beloit Poetry Journal*, *Cerise Press*, *Drunken Boat*, *Four Centuries*, *Hinchas de Poesie*, *Hungarian Review*, *MayDay*, *New Review of Literature*, *Poetry Salzburg Review*, *Otoliths*, *Shofar*, *Metamorphosis*, *OPEN*, *Stolen Island Review*, and *World Literature Today*.

Valdez Hill is a classical pianist who seamlessly blends music and poetry in his creative work. He is the Founder and Artistic Director of *Giving Concerts*. Valdez's poetry career has quickly gained recognition—his first two poems, *"Leda and the Swan"* (a response to the well-known work by William Butler Yeats) and *"A Symphony of Sound and Fear"*, were published in the Moonstone Arts Center anthologies *Remembering William Butler Yeats*

(June 8, 2025) and *Go Back Where You Came From* (July 1, 2025), respectively. Another of his poems was featured in Verseve's *Stars Anthology* (October 5, 2025). His poetry has been read at numerous art galleries and cultural events, and several local artists have commissioned his work. Additionally, two of his haiku poems reached the finals of the *Best Haiku 2025* international anthology by *Haiku Crush* and are slated for publication in December 2025. Beyond writing and performing, Valdez has shared his passion for poetry as a guest lecturer, teaching two poetry classes at Crystal Middle School in the Fairfield-Suisun Unified School District.

Vivian Faith Prescott was born and raised on the island of Ḵaachx̱aana.áak'w, Wrangell, Alaska, in the Alexander Archipelago where she lives and writes at her fishcamp. She's a member of the Pacific Sámi Searvi (Indigenous Sámi diaspora) and a founding member of Community Roots, the first LGBTQIA group on the island. Vivian facilitates two Alaskan writers' groups: the Blue Canoe Writers and the Drumlin Poets. She's the author of 14 books, including poetry, fiction, and non-fiction.

Arika Hendren lives in Salem, Oregon where she teaches nearby. She has many hobbies and interests but was recently inspired by the early songs of Bob Dylan, such as: "Blowin' in the Wind," "The Times They Are A-Changin'," and "Masters of War." Feeling the correlation between those times and these, she composed a series of poems reflecting feelings about the current political climate and social justice.

Sally Sultzman was a reader first, a writer second, but always a storyteller. She's been published with Cast of Wonders, Tales of Sley House, Die Laughing, Luna Station Quarterly and Not a Pipe Publishing as well as the anthology Disability in Dystopia and the anthology To Appalachia With Love, which she also edited as Sarah STETS. A member of SFWA, she lives in rural Illinois with her family, her rescue dog, and a collection of oversized tea mugs. Find out more at www.sallysultzman.com.

Shikhandin is the pen name of an Indian author. Her published books include, *Impetuous Women* (Penguin-Random House India), *Immoderate Men* (Speaking Tiger), *The Woman on the Red Oxide Floor* (Red River Story, India), *After Grief – Poems* (Red River, India), and *Vibhuti Cat* (Duckbill-Penguin-Random House India). In 2024 she was

shortlisted for the Asian Prize for Short Fiction and was a finalist for Himal Fiction Fest (*Himal Magazine*) in 2025. She is a two times Pushcart nominee – Aeolian Harp 2019 (USA) and Cha: An Asian Literary Journal 2011 (Hong Kong), and a Best of the Net nominee – Yellow Arrow Publishing 2023 (USA). Her other honours include, runner up - George Floyd Short Story Contest 2020 (UK), winner - Children First Contest curated by Duckbill in association with Parag an initiative of Tata Trust in 2017, first prize - Brilliant Flash Fiction Contest 2019 (USA), runner up - Erbacce Poetry Prize 2018 (UK), winner 35th Moon Prize (Writing in a Woman's Voice: USA). Shikhandin's prose and poetry have been widely published in India and abroad in online and print journals and anthologies.

Jonathan Fletcher holds a Master of Fine Arts in Creative Writing from Columbia University School of the Arts. His work has been featured in numerous literary journals and magazines, and he has won or placed in various literary contests. A Pushcart Prize, Best of the Net, and Best Microfiction nominee, he won Northwestern University Press's Drinking Gourd Chapbook Poetry Prize contest in 2023, for which his debut chapbook, *This is My Body*, was published in 2025. Currently, he serves as a Zoeglossia Fellow and lives in San Antonio, Texas.

Lisa Meece might be ready to admit she's an artist, but then again, she might not be ready quite yet. Ready or not menopause is reminding her that her time is limited, and the birth of her first granddaughter, Viviene Sage, is reminding her that things can be messy and still beautiful, and giving her courage that overcomes her fear. Her poetry has been published in a couple of anthologies. She hosts the Starbase Indy Podcast, where she talks to people inspired by science fiction to work toward hopeful futures in the real world. She also creates 3d print designs that can be found on Thingiverse under the username fightfascism

Kevin Mack is a disabled combat veteran and retired Air Force pilot. He writes speculative fiction, often--but not always--within an historical setting. An alumnus of the Futurescapes Writing Workshop and the Sandia Starforgers Retreat, he can be found on Bluesky @kevin-mack.bsky.social

R.J. Huneke is a New York-born author and exile living in Portugal. He began his writing career as a journalist at *Newsday*, *Gadizmo*, and *The Examiner*. At age 19, R.J. traveled across the U.S. from New York to California in a dilapidated van with no brakes or heat in the winter and began to write the first of more than ten novels. The proud autistic artist's newest book is a fairy tale-noir titled *Ants Waking* and his cyberpunk-tinged thriller novel *Cyberwar* was published worldwide in 2015; along with a bevy of creative projects, he is the founder of TheForgottenFiction Magazine, and a contributor to the Science Fiction and Fantasy Writers Association [sfwa.org]. He currently lives with his wife, their daughter, a spotted dog, and an unspotted cat in northern Portugal.

Dale Patrick Smrekar is a Florida based satirical writer who takes common everyday subjects and turns them upside down to create new perspectives of commonly held beliefs or mythological entities. Like Santa Claus is a hit man in the off season in *Santa Claus is Coming to Town*. There are no sacred cows in his world. Dale recently graduated with a M.A. in Creative Writing from St. Leo University. In real life he is a certified personal property appraiser and high-end liquidator and owner of a twenty-four-year-old company, Downsizing Advisory Service, which helps people avoid getting taken advantage of when selling their antiques and jewelry. He is retiring this December to fulfil his dream of becoming a full-time writer.

Kurt Newton (he/him) has been writing poetry for most his adult life, some even earlier. His poem "Koala Bear Underwear" in the fifth grade was a big hit among classmates. His interest in politics goes way back to before he was born. His mother was a volunteer on the campaign to elect John F. Kennedy. Kurt's more recent political commentaries can be found in *More Alternative Truths, Alternative Truths: Endgame* and at *Eye to the Telescope*. His writing life (among other things) is on display at Facebook. Send him a friend request; he could use it.

Adam J. Galanski-De León is a writer from Chicago, IL. He is the author of the short story collection, "The Laughter of Hyenas at Bay" (Raging Opossum Press), and the novel, "Szarotka" (American Buffalo Books). He maintains a website at http://www.adamjgalanskideleon.com.

Karen Eisenbrey (she/her) lives in Seattle, WA, where she leads a quiet, orderly life and invents stories to make up for it. She's the author of the *Daughter of Magic* trilogy (*Daughter of Magic, Wizard Girl,* and *Death's Midwife*), the *St. Rage* series (*The Gospel According to St. Rage, Barbara and the Rage Brigade,* and *Far from Normal*), *Ego & Endurance,* and *Tales From Deep River, Book 1: A Quest for Hidden Things* and *Book 2: Deep River Rising*. She also sings in a church choir and plays drums in a garage band. Find more info on Karen's books and short fiction, follow her band-name blog, and sign up for her quarterly newsletter at kareneisenbreywriter.com

Christopher Woods is a writer and photographer who lives in Texas. He has published a novel, *The Dream Patch*, a prose collection, *Under A Riverbed Sky*, and a poetry collection, *Maybe Birds Would Carry It Away*. His novella, *Hearts in The Dark*, was published in an anthology by *Running Wild Press* in Los Angeles. He has received residencies from The Ucross Foundation and the Edward Albee Foundation, and a grant from the Mary Roberts Rinehart Foundation. His plays included *Moonbirds*, an absurdist play about census-takers in a country where there are no people left to count, *Fire*, a drama about a woman who loses her family in a house fire she may have set, *Interim*, about souls in Purgatory, and *Heart Speak*, an evening of monologues for men and women.

Gallery -https://christopherwoods.zenfolio.com/f861509283

Mark Wyatt spent most of his career teaching in South and South-East Asia and the Middle East, where he engaged intensely in academic research, producing numerous articles related to English language teacher education, and several co-edited books. Since returning to the UK two years ago, he has focused primarily on  producing pattern poetry and he discusses his techniques in 'Using letters as number-like particles in constructing pattern poetry', an article that appeared in the *Journal of Mathematics and the Arts*. His poems, many inspired by Ovid's *Metamorphoses*, often adopting the personae of the disenfranchised, have recently appeared in various magazines, including *Artemis Journal, Borderless, Cosmic Daffodil, Dust Poetry, Exterminating Angel, Full Bleed, Greyhound Journal, Hyperbolic Review, Ink Sweat and Tears, Libre, MacQueen's Quinterly, Neologism Poetry Journal, Osmosis, The Plentitudes, Radon Journal, Re-Mediate, Shift, Sontag Mag, Streetcake Magazine, Talking About Strawberries All Of The Time, Tap Into Poetry, Tupelo Quarterly,* and *Typo*.

Benjamin Gorman (he/him) is an award-winning teacher, political activist, author, poet, and publisher at Not a Pipe Publishing. He's an author-in-exile living in Barcelona, Spain with bibliophile and guillotine aficionado Chrys, their kid Franke, three dogs, and two cats. His novels are *The Sum of Our Gods*, *Corporate High School*, *The Digital Storm*, and *The Convention of Fiends* series: *Don't Read This Book*, *You Were Warned*, and *You People Are Monsters*. He's also the

author of two books of poetry, *When She Leaves Me* and *This Uneven Universe*, and the non-fiction book *Dear America: A Breakup Letter*.

M.R. Lehman Wiens is a Pushcart-nominated writer and stay-at-home dad living in Minnesota. His work has previously appeared, or is upcoming in, *F(r)iction*, *Short Édition*, *Consequence*, *The Wild Umbrella Literary Journal*, and others. He can be found at lehmanwienswrites.com.

Myles Gordon is a writer living in Massachusetts.

Leah Mueller work is published in *Rattle, Certain Age, Beach Chair Press, NonBinary Review, Brilliant Flash Fiction, New Flash Fiction Review, Does It Have Pockets, Outlook Springs, Your Impossible Voice*, etc. She has received several nominations for Pushcart and Best of the Net. One of her short stories appears in the 2022 edition of *Best Small Fictions*. Her fourteenth book, *A Pretty Good Disaster* was published by Alien Buddha Press in 2025. Check out more of her work at substack.com/@leahsnapdragon.

Adam C Lipscomb (he/him) is in all probability a carbon-based life form living with his partner and two Very Good Dogs in Decatur, GA. His work has been published in the Seattle Erotic Art Festival's 2020 Literary Art Anthology, Celestite Poetry Journal, and the Pine Cone Review. He has two self-published chapbooks, "Songs of Love and Loss" and "The Gift of Forgetting," both available at Bookshop.org.

When not glaring in frustration at a computer monitor trying to will words to appear, he enjoys cooking for the people in his heart and taking long, romantic walks to the taco truck.

Joanna Michal Hoyt (she/her) is a community volunteer, farmer, baker, and writer who tries stubbornly to see and serve God in everyone. Having grown up in a conservative Christian homeschool group and a progressive unschool group, she knows and loves people on multiple sides of the country's deep divides. She's lived and worked with communities that farmed sustainably, welcomed refugees and migrants, and tried to help neighbors in rural New York State and rural Georgia, and now she lives and works at a Massachusetts farm which is also a residential treatment center for adults dealing with major mental illnesses. Read more of her speculative and historical fiction, often preoccupied with faith, fear, the edges of rationality and the things that connect us across divides, through links from https://joannamichalhoyt.com/